*Fabulous Fathers*

### *"It's my Daddy List," Cory told Nathan in a small voice.*

"Mommy and me, we're looking for a daddy. Someone to marry us and live with us forever. We need a daddy real bad."

Nathan's heart did a somersault. "You need a daddy," he repeated, as if realizing it for the first time. "Well, son," he whispered, "I hope you get the very best daddy in the world. Because any man would be lucky to have a boy like you."

"Then—" Cory swallowed "—then would you—"

"Cory," Faith said quickly, "we talked about this, remember, and I told you—"

"I know you said that Nathan could not be my daddy, but—but you always say you'll never know if you don't ask."

Dear Reader,

Ah, summertime...those lazy afternoons and sultry nights. The perfect time to find romance with a mysterious stranger in a far-off land, or right in your own backyard—with an irresistible Silhouette Romance hero. Like Nathan Murphy, this month's FABULOUS FATHER. Nathan had no interest in becoming a family man, but when Faith Reynolds's son, Cory, showed him *The Daddy List*, Nathan couldn't help losing his heart to the boy, and his pretty mom.

The thrills continue as two strong-willed men show their women how to trust in love. Elizabeth August spins a stirring tale for ALWAYS A BRIDESMAID! in *The Bridal Shower*. When Mike Flint heard that Emma Wynn was about to marry another man, he was determined to know if her love for him was truly gone, or burning deep within. In Laura Anthony's *Raleigh and the Rancher* for WRANGLERS AND LACE, ranch hand Raleigh Travers tries her best to resist ranch owner Daniel McClintock. Can Daniel's love help Raleigh forget her unhappy past?

Sometimes the sweetest passions can be found right next door, or literally on your doorstep, as in Elizabeth Sites's touching story *Stranger in Her Arms* and the fun-filled *Bachelor Blues* by favorite author Carolyn Zane.

Natalie Patrick makes her writing debut with the heartwarming *Wedding Bells and Diaper Pins*. Winning custody of her infant godson seemed a lost cause for Dani McAdams until ex-fiancé Matt Taylor offered a marriage of convenience. But unexpected feelings between them soon began to complicate their convenient arrangement!

Happy Reading!

Anne Canadeo
Senior Editor

Please address questions and book requests to:
Silhouette Reader Service
U.S.: 3010 Walden Ave., P.O. Box 1325, Buffalo, NY 14269
Canadian: P.O. Box 609, Fort Erie, Ont. L2A 5X3

# THE DADDY LIST

## Myrna Mackenzie

Silhouette
ROMANCE™
Published by Silhouette Books
America's Publisher of Contemporary Romance

For Brad and Ross, my sons—
You light up my world with your noise and your laughter.
Each day is an adventure, filled with joy and the magic of
looking at life through your eyes.

 SILHOUETTE BOOKS

ISBN 0-373-19090-5

THE DADDY LIST

This edition published by arrangement with Harlequin Enterprises B.V.

® and TM are trademarks of Harlequin Enterprises B.V., used under
license. Trademarks indicated with ® are registered in the United States
Patent and Trademark Office, the Canadian Trade Marks Office and in
other countries.

**Printed in U.S.A.**

**Books by Myrna Mackenzie**

Silhouette Romance

*The Baby Wish* #1046
*The Daddy List* #1090

## MYRNA MACKENZIE

has always been fascinated by the belief that within every man is a hero, inside every woman lives a heroine. She loves to write about ordinary people making extraordinary dreams come true. A former teacher, Myrna lives in Illinois with her husband—who was her high school sweatheart—and two sons, and is the sole caretaker for a goldfish named Billy.

### *Nathan Murphy on Fatherhood…*

Cory,

When you came into my life, I didn't want you there, but…there you were and there was nothing I could do.

You hit me like a rocket, you and that list of yours. What other kid in the whole world could ever be like you? What other kid would make a list of all the things he wanted in a daddy and then go searching for one?

You're truly special to me, Cory. I care for you, and I would never want to hurt you or your mom. But I'm afraid I may not be the man who can fulfill your list.

You and your mother deserve only the best. It's what I want for both of you—the very best dad and husband in the world. It's what I wish I could be. But since I don't think that's possible, I want you to know I'll always be your friend.

Nathan

# Chapter One

Her four-year-old son was absolutely right, Faith Reynolds thought, looking at her watch and realizing that she was late for her appointment. It *was* a burnt bacon kind of day.

Blowing out a puff of air that lifted her bangs, she gripped the steering wheel more firmly and lightly pressed down on the accelerator, trying to make up for lost time.

The day had started out nicely enough she thought as she drove along. Blue sky, sunshine. Faith remembered thinking that something wonderful was bound to happen on such a day. But that was before Cory had picked up a spoonful of oatmeal and told her that he wanted to tell her "somepin' important."

"Billy Wilkins' daddy is coming for show-and-tell at preschool today," he'd said, studying her with dark, earnest eyes.

And the sky had suddenly lost some of its blue. Faith lost

the urge to eat anything at all. She reached out and brushed back his sleep-tousled hair.

"I could come for show-and-tell if you let me know in advance," she offered softly.

Cory stirred his spoon through the oatmeal, making circular tracks for the milk to fill in. "You came, Mom. You did. 'Member?"

She nodded, unable to ignore the lump that was growing in her throat. She wanted so badly for him to have all he needed. No, she wanted to be able to *be* everything he needed.

"We could ask Mandy to come for show-and-tell," she said.

Cory let go of his spoon, leaving it anchored in the sticky cereal. He shifted on his chair. "Baby-sitters do not make good show-and-tell," he told her. "And Scotty Miller's daddy is coming next week."

"I see. And you want to bring a daddy, too, don't you?" It was no good ignoring the situation; there was no joy in letting him struggle to the painful point himself.

But Cory sat silent, sucking at his lip. His eyes were round and he held himself very still. Even his bare feet that poked out of the legs of his pajamas were motionless, not pumping back and forth like they usually were.

It was the moment Faith had always feared, the someday when her child would feel different. Left out.

"Do you think you'll ever get me a daddy?" he'd asked in a voice that was much smaller, more strained than the Cory voice she was used to.

*No*, Faith had wanted to scream. *You had a daddy once and he didn't want us, he threw us away. I wouldn't ever risk feeling that way about anyone again, couldn't stand that kind of hurt and humiliation for you or for me.*

But of course, she couldn't say that. She'd worked so hard to make Cory believe that he had been loved all the way around. And in truth, she wanted a father for him. It was what she herself had always wanted as a child, a daddy of her own. And it was time to face the facts; not all marriages were based on strong and scary feelings. There were people who married with more practical intentions; like common interests, mutual benefit, to obtain a father for a child.

"*Do* you think I'll ever have a daddy, Mom?" Cory asked again.

Faith stared at him long and hard, biting her lip, ignoring her cooling cup of coffee. "I don't know yet, Cory. We'll have to see. I'll think about it. I promise."

But as they sat there studying her words, the smoke alarm had brought them out of the trance. Faith had scurried to save the unsalvageable bacon. Cory had tried to open a window until Faith had told him to sit down while she took care of everything.

It *was*, indeed, a burnt bacon kind of day. And it had only gone downhill since then.

Now, turning the wheel of the car, Faith headed down a rutted lane. After fifteen minutes of passing nothing but fields of grass and newborn dandelions, she realized that she had managed to miss the house she was looking for. Again.

Running one hand through her long hair, she slowly pulled over and looked at the spidery handwritten map Dr. Anderson had given her. Staring more carefully, she realized that the number she'd been reading as a one was, in fact, a seven. And the words that had looked like Hiller Road, could, by a long stretch of the imagination, also be interpreted as Hidden Road.

"It figures," she said to no one in particular, and suddenly the whole frustrating situation seemed rather funny. She'd started the day thinking that something wonderful was going to happen, and here she sat, miles from her destination, visiting with the dandelions. Not that dandelions were so awful; their buttery yellow heads had never seemed deserving of the term *weed* in Faith's eyes. Still, she *was* in the wrong place. Nathan Murphy's house was nowhere near, and she was going to have some explaining to do when she got there. Which was too bad, since she'd already been warned that the man had raised hell when he'd heard that she was coming.

The thought alone made her squirm. She didn't want Nathan Murphy to be her patient any more than he wanted her to be his physical therapist. The man had once been Southeastern Illinois Memorial's top surgeon, a genius it was said, a man with magic in his fingertips. And she was sorry his hands were injured, that his career had been ended in an auto accident that had taken the lives of his wife and daughter well over a year ago. But she had a full caseload of patients, people who needed her, who were in the midst of treatment. She had no room for another patient, especially one who'd put off therapy and who would need extended sessions. At least those were the words she'd told her supervisor and Dr. Anderson. Though she knew there was more.

She'd met Nathan Murphy once before, soon after she'd joined the staff, and had been instantly spooked by her response to him. He'd barely said a word, barely noticed her and yet, when she'd looked into his eyes, her heart had raced, her breath had quickened, and fifty-foot Danger signals had flashed red before her eyes—until she'd seen the ring on his left hand and sweet relief had rushed through her veins.

But that had been two years ago, when he'd been a married man. Safe. Off-limits. Now things had changed. Or some things had. Faith still shied away from emotional encounters, she didn't risk letting her feelings get involved in any way, with anyone. No way would she have taken on this case had she been given a choice. But there had been no choice. Dr. Anderson had made it clear that she was to be Nathan Murphy's therapist, that this was an assignment she would not be allowed to turn away from.

And now she was late. Not quite lost, but late.

Faith shrugged and turned the car around. "I guess you can't win on a burnt bacon kind of day," she said at last. She wondered if Nathan Murphy understood about those kinds of days. But then he'd have to, wouldn't he? With his surgeon's hands injured, stiffened and useless, he'd had many burnt bacon kinds of days in the past year and a half. Far more than she had.

Suddenly Faith felt chastened, ashamed of her own frustration. After all, it wasn't Nathan's fault that she'd had a bad day, that she already had too many patients, or that he was an unwelcome reminder of her past mistakes.

In just a short while, *her* day was going to improve. She'd be home with Cory. They'd laugh and cuddle, talk about little things, silly things, big things; maybe even discuss finding a father for him. Initiating a practical, unemotional search for a man who wanted a wife and a little boy of his own. Things would work out and soon her world would be bright and blue again.

But Nathan Murphy had a longer road ahead of him.

A *hidden* road, she thought, looking down at the map once again. In more ways than one.

Still, she couldn't take that kind of a defeatist attitude. She had a job to do, a commitment to fulfill. And her task right now was to find the man's house, examine him, set up a workable schedule.

Her job was to establish a simple patient-therapist relationship... and to block out any memory of the way she'd felt the first time she'd ever met the man.

Nathan sat in his near empty house, listening to the monotonous tick of the clock. Like water dripping out of a leaky faucet, the sound irritated, kept his thoughts from wandering where they wanted to, kept him in the present, and reminded him of... something. Something he was supposed to remember. What was it?

Oh yeah, today was the day Anderson was sending the physical therapist, the best money could buy, he'd said. She was coming... when? Forty-five minutes ago.

Closing his eyes, Nathan let out a long, slow breath, let his head fall back against the cushioned chair. Good. Anderson must have forgotten. Bad enough that the man had stormed in here two days ago bellowing that Nathan had grieved and neglected himself long enough, demanding that Nathan get on with his life. Bad enough that the man had insisted that it was his right as a friend to tell Nathan he'd spent too much time wallowing in self-pity.

Then the damn man had gone and said he was sending a therapist, like it or not. That he would take whatever steps necessary, legal or otherwise, to ensure that Nathan opted for treatment, that he was through leaving him alone—unless Nathan made the right choice and gave in to the inevitable.

He'd even threatened to call Celine, Nathan's sister. His sweet, loving, emotional sister, the sister he'd lied to for over a year, reassuring her, telling her he was fine. If Anderson called her, she'd be packed in a heartbeat. She'd come and cry, she'd want to talk about Amy and Joanna, relive memories Nathan had spent months trying to bury. She'd dredge it all up, and worse, she'd bring her family, her five little ones that Amy had played with. She'd bring buckets of love and tears and children, things he couldn't deal with, wouldn't allow himself anymore. And he'd hurt her in his desperation to have her gone. Just seeing what he'd become would wound her. He couldn't risk that. And that was what Anderson had threatened, poking around Nathan's house, studying Nathan, seeing how he was these days.

Nathan hadn't doubted that Dan Anderson would do just as he said. He was a tough doctor, a tough man. He was a terrible pain in the rear end even if he did happen to be a friend. But thankfully, he was also busy right now and had obviously forgotten to send the therapist.

Good, Nathan thought. It would save him the trouble of throwing her out.

It would keep him from having to argue that none of Anderson's lofty plans would change a thing. They wouldn't bring Nathan's wife and daughter back to life. They couldn't erase what had already happened. Because even if Anderson and his therapist worked a miracle and gave him back his hands tomorrow, even if he went on to save a life a day for the rest of his own days, that wouldn't make a damn bit of difference to him. He would still hear his daughter's cries in the night, still wake up sweat soaked and shaking in the dark . . . just as he deserved to.

No, nothing would change. And he didn't want it to. He didn't want a damn therapist or a second chance. All he wanted was to be left alone. Completely alone.

The doorbell rang, two long peals, shredding the silence. Damn. She was late, but she was here. It had to be her. No one else but Anderson was foolish enough to come around anymore. And Dan would be at the hospital now.

Nathan rose, went to the front door, stood looking at the slippery doorknob. He made no attempt to touch it.

"It's open," he said, standing to one side. Of course it was always open. He couldn't manage the nightmarish lock mechanism, wouldn't have even if he could. What was the point in keeping out the bogeyman when he was on speaking terms with his own personal demons?

But then the door opened, and all thought of locks and doorknobs and demons drained away. A woman stood there in the tunnel of sunlight that streamed through the open door. She had long, honey brown curls. Curls that the wind had tossed about her face. Nathan noticed that the top of her head barely cleared his shoulders. He also noticed that while she was smiling, her blue green eyes were wary.

The wariness was something, a tool, Nathan could use. Dan Anderson thought he had Nathan under his thumb, but he'd bet that Dan hadn't witnessed those worried blue green eyes firsthand. If this was the best Southeastern Illinois Memorial had to offer, then he was home free. She'd be running back to Dan inside of five minutes.

A thread of a smile made its way to Nathan's face. At least that was the way it felt. He knew it wasn't real. Smiles weren't a part of his life anymore.

But she was still looking up at him, still smiling. "Dr. Murphy, hello. I'm Faith Reynolds. Dr. Anderson told me that he'd spoken to you."

"You might say that." Nathan didn't step aside or invite her farther into the room. He would have liked to cross his arms, something that might have suggested menace, but that only would have called attention to the fact that his fingers no longer folded around his biceps, no longer bent at all. Instead he leaned on the narrow edge of the open door, one arm hidden. With some difficulty, he managed to shove the stiff thumb of the other hand through the back belt loop of his jeans. He leaned forward into Faith Reynold's face.

"You and Dan must have gotten your signals mixed, Ms. Reynolds. No way did I ask for a therapist."

By Nathan's calculations, she should have taken a step backward right around now. He was taller than her, bigger than her, and he was in her space. He was crowding her.

Instead, she turned the wattage up on her smile. He could almost feel the heat on his face. That's how lit up she looked. But in the small *V* of delicate peach-tinted skin at her throat, Nathan saw that her pulse had kicked up the pace a touch—three heartbeats faster, maybe four. It wasn't what he'd hoped for, but it was something.

"I know you didn't ask for a therapist, Dr. Murphy. Dr. Anderson made the situation very clear. You don't want a therapist. But I'm afraid you've got one."

She lifted one small shoulder in a tiny shrug. "By the way, I *am* sorry I'm late, but I made a few wrong turns. You really live pretty far from civilization, don't you?"

Ignoring the fact that he was still a breath away from her face, she slipped out from beneath his glare and moved into the room.

Nathan turned as she passed him. He still hadn't closed the door. He didn't intend to. At least not until this petite and unwelcome woman had gone back to where she came from.

He watched in amazement as she moved to the curtains, the ones he never opened. Pulling on the drawstring, she drew them wide, letting in the outside, and more light than he'd seen in a long time.

Nathan felt the heat rising within him. He didn't bother trying to tamp it down.

"I thought I made myself clear, lady," he said, straightening to his full six feet. "I want you gone from here. Now. No matter what Dan told you, this is my body, my life, my house. I didn't invite you, and I sure as hell don't have to have you."

Her face was turned slightly toward the window, though she heard him well enough. He could see it in the way her lips trembled slightly. And he noticed her lips because errant strands of her hair had caught on them, tawny wisps that she brushed away with her fingers, like a child dusting chocolate bits from a candy-smeared mouth. She shoved her hair away from her face, and the movement called attention to the small, pale earlobe that had been hidden before. He suddenly wished she was bigger, meaner looking, with thin lips and cold eyes. He wished she'd put all that honey-toned hair in a bun, hide it under a hat, chop it off. He wished she'd get out of here. Fast.

"It's so green here," she said wistfully, gazing out at the trees surrounding his house, totally ignoring his request that she leave. "My son would love this place. He's just four, and there's so much room to run. A kid's paradise. It's fresh—almost wild. Is that what attracted you to it?"

The mention of her son cut through Nathan, snapping whatever human feelings and concerns he'd had, stealing her protection. So what if she was small and fragile? She was all that he didn't want to deal with. A therapist, someone who would try to help him when the last thing he wanted was to be helped. A woman, one who was delicate, soft and pretty, with a voice like silk on naked flesh. A reminder of what he'd lost in more ways than one. A woman with a small child.

"I live here because I want to be left alone, and no one comes out this far to bother me, Ms. Reynolds. Understand?"

He didn't wait for her answer, just nodded toward the outside when she turned to look at him fully. "Here's the door," he said. "I'll tell Dan that you showed up. We wouldn't want any black marks on that silvery reputation you've made for yourself, would we? Don't worry, I won't tell him anything but the truth. You came, I wasn't buying, and I sent you packing. End of story."

She stood there, taking deep breaths. Her chin had risen a solid notch or two, and she hadn't taken one single step from her place by the window.

"The door," he reminded her softly. The edge in his voice was real. Other than Dan, Nathan didn't talk to anyone much anymore, and it was entirely by choice. He didn't want anyone around. He especially didn't want to stand around chatting about how green the grass was. No, he didn't want to talk about a blasted thing. Not with this woman.

He leaned against the door, opening it wider, just as if that little bit of a body wouldn't fit through the already yawning opening. Pulling his arm around, he gestured toward her car out in the drive.

Her eyes lit instantly on his hand. In his anger he'd forgotten to hide the long, unyielding fingers. Now they hung in midair, open to her for several seconds before he stuffed the hand into his armpit. "You can leave anytime now," he said. "Like I said, here's the door. You do understand the words *I don't want you here*, don't you?"

"Of course, Dr. Murphy, and I do know where the door is," she said softly. "And that you'd like to close it in my face. But I also know that it opens easily, that you don't lock it. And even if you did—" she smiled suddenly, smugly, her eyes widening "—even if you did lock the door, I have a key," she told him, fishing one out of the back pocket of her work whites.

Nathan stood there, breathing deeply. If he'd been any hotter, flames would have been streaming from his nostrils. He couldn't believe that Dan had even given this stranger, this woman, a key to his house.

"Don't bother raising your voice," she told him. "I'm used to dealing with difficult patients, Dr. Murphy. It's part of my job. And Dr. Anderson warned me about you, don't worry. You can't do anything to blacken my reputation. Only I can. And I could only do that if I let you run me off. But I'm not going to."

As if to prove her point, she plopped down on the dusty couch, stifling a sneeze. Nodding toward the other end, she motioned for him to sit down. "Now, if you've finished arguing, Dr. Murphy, we've got things to talk about."

Amazed at her stubbornness, unsure how to get her out of here, short of calling the police or...hurting her, Nathan swore beneath his breath. Turning on his heel, he left the room. If he couldn't get rid of her, he'd ignore her. Sooner or later, she'd get the hint.

But he could hear the soft slide of rubber-soled shoes behind him. Turning quickly, he caught her nose square in the middle of his chest. His arms reached out to catch her, then he froze, taking one long stride back.

"You'd better have a damn good reason for tailing me, short stuff. What does it take for you to get the message? A telegram from the president? Can't you see that I want to be left the hell alone?"

She was biting her lip, breathing deeply as if she'd just run a race. Her cheeks were flushed, her hair was tumbled from her collision with him.

"Now we're getting somewhere," she said suddenly. "*You* want to be left alone, and *I'm* absolutely prepared to get out of your life forever."

He waited. It was clear by the smug smile on her gorgeous little lips that she was preparing to spring the trap.

"And when will that lucky day be?" he asked.

"When you're back in shape, one hundred percent. When you no longer feel you have to hide your hands behind your back."

Slowly, with an eerie smile that he didn't mean, Nathan drew both his hands out and held them up before her face.

She stared at them, giving each a clinical appraisal, then shook her head slowly. "Bringing them out for shock effect or just to get rid of me doesn't cut it, Murphy. You'll get me out of your life once and for all, forever, when they actually do the job they're meant to do. I'll do the supreme vanishing act when you're back in the operating arena. That's the deal. You give me flack, cause me grief, slow down your progress and you'll have me just that much longer. You try to keep me out, I'll sic Dr. Anderson and the whole ever-loving hospital administration on you. You're top priority, don't you know? And you don't have a choice in this matter. Neither do I."

Her words gave him pause. He hadn't considered the fact that she wasn't a willing participant in this fiasco. But then, why should that matter to him?

"Is Dan forcing this on you?" he demanded, shoving his hands back behind his back.

Faith raised her head quickly, looking him dead in the eye. "This is a job, Dr. Murphy. You've been assigned to me, no ifs, ands or buts. And I'll admit that it's an inconvenience. I already have a full complement of patients, people who are counting on me, people who aren't ordering me out the door. A little boy who's taking the first steps he's managed in a year. A woman who's just starting to believe she won't be a burden to her family. I don't really have the time or the inclination for a royal pain in the bottom like you, who doesn't even want my help. But I've got you, anyway. And I don't argue when my orders come. I love my work, but it's also my bread and butter. If I don't work, we don't eat."

Nathan didn't have to ask who "we" was. With her hands outstretched, he could clearly see the bracelet that slipped down her wrist. Made of macaroni bits that had obviously been spray painted red, it was held together with a frayed bit of blue yarn. There were spots where the paint had either not adhered or had chipped away, leaving yellow shadows here and there. Not an attractive piece of jewelry by a long shot; yet she wore it. And Nathan knew why—instantly.

The bracelet had been made by a child, her son. It screamed "family" like a siren in the dead of night. And family was a word Nathan shied away from, dreaded; one that crept up on him in dreams that started out sweet and turned bitter and haunting before the night was over. One more reason he didn't want Faith Reynolds around. She had a child, valued him, wore his treasures for all the world to see. Never mind all the rest. Never mind the lady herself. The woman was taboo with a capital *T*.

Faith studied Nathan as he turned from her, blowing out a breath. One hand still rested somewhere behind him, the other raked at his blond hair with fingers that no longer functioned properly. His green eyes were narrowed, his chin jutted out as if preparing for one more fight with her.

She could have told him that it was pointless. With Dr. Anderson geared up and breathing fire, Nathan Murphy had become top priority at the hospital. They'd given him time, valuable time in therapy terms, to mourn and come about. Now they were prepared to drag him kicking and screaming back into the world of the living. He was too precious a commodity for the administration to waste,

Anderson had insisted. Murphy and his magical fingers was the shot in the arm that the financially troubled Southeastern Illinois Memorial needed. A big hitter. A name to be brought in. By Faith.

There was a lot riding on her success with this man. Her own reputation was at stake. That was why she was here.

But was it why she was staying? Partly, she knew, and partly, because of something else. Looking up into Nathan Murphy's eyes in those first few seconds, Faith had suffered a shock. She'd dealt with many patients, was used to seeing the lights of people's souls dimmed. She was used to fear and frustration, anger and bitterness on the part of her patients. Somehow it was still frightening to see *this* man like that. She remembered looking up at him two years ago, remembered feeling as if she'd just touched a live wire. Nathan was too full of life to get close to. She'd heard other people say the same. But this Nathan, this new Nathan...Faith couldn't finish the thought. The old Nathan might have been dangerous, but at least he had been alive.

She knew just what was driving Dr. Anderson...why he was pushing so hard. Because Faith wanted to know that Dr. Murphy was back, alive and working his miracles with his magical hands, too. And even though she didn't want to be the one to bring him back, she could no more walk away from him than she could stop the flow of day and night.

"You haven't spoken for several minutes, Ms. Reynolds. It couldn't be that you've come up with a way out of this for both of us, could it?"

He was still looking away, as if he couldn't bear to stare at her anymore. And with his head turned to the side, Faith could see just how long and shaggy his dark blond hair had grown. She wondered if the length of his hair was simply part and parcel of the fact that he no longer took care of himself properly or if it was more a reflection of the rebel within him. For there was no doubt in her mind that Nathan Murphy *was* a rebel. He probably worked his magic on patients by threatening them if they didn't get well.

She looked at his hands, at his long, stiffened fingers that had saved so many lives, healed so many helpless people. "No way on earth have I changed my mind, doctor."

He turned to her then, his voice deadly. "I'm not going to the hospital for treatment, no matter what you threaten me with, Ms. Reynolds. Nobody, not you, not Dan, is going to drag me in there so that everyone can gawk at me. I value my privacy."

"So you told me." Faith tilted her head. "And I told *you* that I had patients scheduled all day long. I'll come here after hours."

Nathan took a step nearer, leaned closer, his eyes level with her own. She knew that he was still trying to intimidate her, trying to get her to back down.

"You have a son, Ms. Reynolds," he reminded her. "One you seem to care about. A kid needs his mother home at night."

She nodded, smiling sweetly into his face. "Yes, I know that, and I'll be there every night after we're done here. While I'm gone, I'll miss Cory very much. He'll be a real incentive for me to get you back in shape quickly. As soon as is humanly and medically possible, we'll be done and I'll be gone."

"Good. I'll send roses on the day you clear out of here, just for the pleasure of seeing you gone."

Something slightly resembling a grim smile passed over Nathan's lips. His eyes which had been narrowed, opened wide, emphasizing his words. For one brief second, Faith stared into those hypnotic, jewel green eyes. The air rushed from her lungs in one swift stream, and she knew without question that once long ago, Nathan *had* been a different man, reckless and wild. That women had thrown their hearts at him whether he asked them to or not, that he'd once used those hands for giving pleasure as well as saving lives.

The thought dropped in like a live grenade.

"Yes, well, Dr. Murphy, I'm sure we'll both look forward to your return to perfect health. I'll just be leaving now. Cory's sitter probably wants to go home. I'll be back as soon as I've made arrangements for a permanent after-hours sitter for him."

She backed away, watching Nathan's eyes, the hard, thin line of his mouth. Swiftly she turned and made for the door. She could hear Nathan's steps behind her.

"Make sure you do get a responsible sitter," he ordered, just as she placed her hand on the still open door.

"What?" Faith whirled at his unexpected words. He was only one step behind her, close, so she had to bend her head back to look into his face.

"A responsible sitter," he repeated. "Don't bring the kid—don't bring him here," he said slowly. His voice was raspy as if he were having difficulty getting the words out. "I can't have a kid here. I don't do the family scene," he said. "It's one thing I won't take any arguments on. All right?"

It was more than a request, more than an order. Nathan's eyes were cold, blanketed, masking the pain she knew she'd find if she looked deep enough. His words were a plea. He'd had a child. He'd lost a child.

Faith understood.

"I'll find someone reliable," she agreed.

For two seconds Faith felt Nathan's gaze burning into her back as she walked away. Then just as quickly, the door closed, severing the contact.

She'd agreed to something she hadn't wanted to do. She'd set the ball rolling with Nathan. But at least she now knew that she needn't worry. Nathan Murphy was well on the way to hating her. What's more, he couldn't ever be around children—or families. It was sad.

It was a godsend.

She would have no trouble maintaining a purely professional relationship with a man like that. She would never have to worry about this man getting too close.

Just a few hours later, Faith got Cory ready for bed. She put the book aside that they'd been reading and pressed a soft kiss on his brow as she arranged his covers.

But Cory sat up straight in bed. Fighting sleep. "Did you think any more about show-and-tell—about my daddy?" he asked.

Folding down a corner of the sheet, smoothing it, Faith nodded. "I have thought about it some, Cory. And I've decided that I would very much like for you to have a daddy. But these things take time, and it's not as simple as you'd think."

"I don't understand," he said, tugging at her hand. "You meet somebody and kiss him real good and smushy. Then you get married. Don't you watch TV, Mom?"

Faith couldn't help the smile that rose to her lips. She wondered what kind of television he was watching during the daytime when she couldn't screen his viewing. But now wasn't the time to belabor that point. Instead, she turned to him with a mock fierce expression. "Cory, you know that television isn't real, don't you?"

Frowning, Cory nodded. "I know. You to'd me once. But how do you find a daddy?"

She didn't have the slightest idea, but there was no way she was going to burst his balloon or his confidence in her.

"Well," Faith leaned close and smoothed the hair back from her son's forehead. She picked up his teddy bear from the foot of the bed and handed it to him. "Maybe we should start by deciding what kind of a man we're looking for. He'd have to be someone we both liked and could live with, you know."

"I know. Daddies are married to moms, too," he agreed. "He'd have to be someone who liked 'sparagus," he said, wrinkling his nose. "Cause you like to cook 'sparagus."

Faith chuckled and nodded. "We wouldn't want him running away in fear of my cooking, that's for sure. But what I meant was, what kind of a person do you think *you'd* want for a daddy? If we're going to look, then we should take our time and be very careful about what we're looking for. And you have to be aware, right up front, that we might not find anyone. It could happen, you know."

She waited, watching him until he raised his chin and looked at her. "I know," he said grudgingly.

"All right, then." Somewhat satisfied that Cory knew the score, Faith took a breath. "So," she said, "you try to describe to me what you think a father should be like."

"Okay." Cory scrambled out of bed. He came back with a storybook—one of his favorites—as well as a torn piece of paper and a stubby pencil with teeth marks on the eraser.

"You write," he said. "Put down, 'The Daddy List' so we don't forget what it is."

Dutifully Faith took the piece of paper and scribbled the words at the top.

"First off," Cory said, "I want him to look like Mr. Benson in this story. I like Mr. Benson. Besides, he looks a lot like me. He's got black hair and brown eyes. I want my daddy to look like me the way Billy Wilkins' daddy does."

"Black hair and brown eyes," Faith repeated, writing the words down.

Cory nodded.

"What else?" Faith asked.

Cory looked at her. He scratched his head and pulled his teddy bear close, fiddling with the nearly defuzzed left ear.

"I don't know. What do you think?" He covered his mouth to hide a yawn and crawled back onto the bed.

Faith smiled, watching her son trying to stay awake. "I think," she said, "that we should think about this when we're both a little more wide awake. After all, we have time. The daddies of the world are not simply going to disappear overnight."

Cory looked uncertain, but as another yawn crept up on him, he nodded his agreement. "Maybe I'll think of some more later. After Scottie's dad comes to school."

Faith smiled and dropped another kiss on Cory's forehead, then tucked him into his bed. As she wandered from the room and quietly shut the door, she looked down at the words on the list she still held in her hand. *Black hair and brown eyes.*

Her first instincts about the day had been right. Several wonderful things had happened. She'd gotten through her interview with Nathan Murphy and came out—well, mostly unscathed. What's more, she and Cory had begun their search for the perfect man.

*Black hair and brown eyes.* It made sense to her.

Tomorrow she'd begin arranging her schedule so that she'd have time for an angry, blond-haired, green-eyed giant. But that wasn't going to be a problem, after all.

Raising the scrap of paper so that the words stood out clearly, Faith read the words once again.

*Black hair and brown eyes.*

Turning to Cory's closed door, she smiled. Her son wanted a father with hair and eyes the color of his own.

It was a wise choice. She guessed she'd just have to do her best to find him what he wanted.

## Chapter Two

If Faith had thought things would be easy just because she and Dr. Murphy had cleared one hurdle, she was apprised of her error the minute she walked through his door the next day.

With an armload of supplies, Faith fumbled for the knob, stumbled into the house and found herself face-to-face with the second button on Nathan's shirt.

She bounced backward two steps and looked up, straight into those fierce green eyes.

"You're late, Ms. Reynolds," he said softly. "Again."

His long, jean-clad legs were spread wide, his arms crossed, emphasizing the chest beneath his white knit shirt. He was a good foot taller than Faith. Most women would have been intimidated. Or intrigued.

But Faith's eyes clung to the vision of his impressive body mere seconds before lighting instead on the awkward spread of his hands that should have been gripping his biceps. He didn't know what to do with those hands, the hands that had once been flexible, talented, capable of performing delicate surgery in spaces that would have made other surgeons blanch. His hands were the only things out of sync with the image of outrage signified by his stance.

"It's nice to know you were worried," she said with a smile, not letting him see the concern that she felt when she looked at those hands.

Nathan's jaw tightened at her flippant words, his eyes narrowed slightly. "Worried isn't the word I'd use. I'm just disappointed that you showed up at all, Ms. Reynolds. I was hoping you'd decided to be reasonable and back off."

"Reasonable?" Faith blinked her eyes wide. "Whatever gave you the idea that I would be reasonable? Good therapists aren't. They're pushy, bossy people who don't know the meaning of the word *quit*. And it's a good thing, too. There are a lot of people dancing tangos today who'd still be confined to wheelchairs if their therapists had been reasonable. Now, hold out your hands."

Nathan stood there looking at her as if she'd just ordered him to drop his pants in public.

"Hold out your hands, Dr. Murphy," she repeated slowly.

"What for?"

"For this," she said, lifting the box she held in her arms. "You need to find a place to put it. I need to get the rest of the equipment out of my car."

Still Nathan didn't move.

"Look, Dr. Murphy, this isn't heavy, and I absolutely promise you there's no dynamite inside. You've got arms, and palms that are flat surfaces. Use them."

With that, Faith practically dropped the box into thin air. To her relief, he reached out automatically and caught it clumsily. Thank goodness. His reflexes were still good.

Besides, she would have had a lot of explaining to do if she'd broken some of the fragile items inside.

But she offered no words of praise for what was, after all, an accomplishment for a man who'd been sitting around vegetating for eighteen months. Faith wasn't sure why. Normally she tried to offer whatever words of encouragement she could, build on every little step. But there was something in Nathan's eyes, his stance—something that told her he wouldn't want her compliments, that he'd back away if she said even one small word. So she didn't. She'd just have to hope that he'd offered himself a mental pat on the back. She'd have to hope that he even cared.

He was making his way to a dusty table, trying to figure out some way to slide the box off of his arms with hands that really had no gripping ability when Faith opened her mouth again.

"By the way, Doctor," she said, turning toward the door. "The reason I was late was because there was an incredible mix-up with my supplies when I went to check them out today. You wouldn't, by any chance, have called the hospital and tried to sabotage my equipment list, would you?"

She glanced back over her shoulder and saw that Nathan had somehow managed to dump the box. He was staring at her, his brow raised, the closest thing she'd seen to a smile lifting one corner of his mouth.

"What do you think, Ms. Reynolds?"

Faith studied him for a full five seconds more, watched the too intense eyes mocking her, daring her to turn and run.

Slowly, she shrugged one shoulder and smiled smugly. "I think that would have been too petty even for someone who dislikes me as much as you do. More likely, it was just typical hospital red tape."

The half smile left his lips. "Believe me, if I'd thought a move like that would have gotten rid of you, I would have tried it."

"That's good to know," she said, opening the door. "Even anger can be good if it gets you up off your backside and doing things. I'll keep that in mind in case you need a nudge sometime during treatment."

Nathan moved with a swiftness that nearly froze Faith's breath in her chest. She took a step back, but even so, when he came to a halt, he was nearly standing on top of her. His warmth and the clean, male scent of him surrounded her, wrapped her in a drugging awareness of him. She could reach out and rake her fingertip across the line of his jaw if she wanted to. His height forced her to tip her head back just to look into his face. And the expression that she saw there wasn't reassuring or kind.

"So nothing shakes you, does it, Ms. Reynolds?" he asked. "I've insulted you, threatened you, and practically shoved you out the door and you stand there telling me that it's good for me to get ticked off. What exactly would it take, I wonder—just how hard would a man have to push— if he wanted to make you run?"

Staring up into Nathan's face, Faith wondered if he knew just how very close she was to bolting right this second. Only necessity and Dr. Anderson's orders were keeping her here. Because every time she stared into Nathan's eyes, saw the pain he tried to blot out with anger, she wanted to run. Badly. Run right out the door and keep on running for the rest of her life.

Those eyes spoke to her, pulled at her, and she didn't want that. She didn't want to feel anything for this man other than a clean-cut professional interest in his treatment. She couldn't feel more than that, wouldn't let herself. And yes, there were definitely things that shook her.

He was one of them. But she'd give up speaking entirely before she'd admit that to Nathan Murphy.

"Excuse me, I'll be back in just a minute," she said, easing away from him, fighting for the breath to force the words out. "There are still a few things in my car. An infrared and paraffin bath. The infrared will serve as an alternate heat source to relax your muscles in case we need it, but I'd rather use the paraffin bath if you can deal with the mess. Don't move, it won't take me long to get the stuff inside."

Nathan let out a long breath. He took a step backward, giving her more space. But his eyes were still angry and lost. His body was still tense.

The few minutes of solitude gave Faith a chance to catch her breath, to get her mind back on track. No one had said this was going to be easy. And anyway, when had anything been easy for her? Ever. Not having had a carefree existence was probably the very thing that made her a good therapist, the thing that made her so independent, made her push. Knowing that there was no one but herself that she could depend on, that there never had and never would be anyone, made her strong, made her take on anything that came her way. Even this job, one she hated. She did it to prove that she could, but she also did it because she had to. So that she could make a better life for her son than she'd had herself.

In time, she'd get past this. Nathan Murphy would be just another patient in a long line of patients. She had to keep telling herself that.

But when she wrestled the last bit of equipment into the house, Faith found that all her good advice about Nathan flew right out the roof. He was slumped in a chair, his long legs stretched out before him, his eyes closed. When she drew near, his lids drifted open and he gifted her with that deadly green stare.

"Is this going to take long, lady?" he demanded.

Faith raised one brow. "Why? Do you have a pressing social engagement? A cocktail party, perhaps?" Her eyes scanned the room. "From the looks of things, you haven't been doing much for the past year or so other than wearing out the cushion on that chair. So I can't imagine what it is you'd be rushing off to. But since your face is beginning to turn a nasty shade of red, I'll answer your question. This *will* take awhile, but I didn't bring my pajamas, if that's what you mean. Therapy isn't a quick trip around the block, Dr. Murphy. Get used to it."

As if her words had hit a nerve, Nathan levered himself out of the chair.

Faith took a step back. She quickly moved to the corner and began setting up the paraffin bath. She could hear Nathan pacing behind her, as if he didn't know quite what to do with himself now that he was no longer sitting down.

"You'll have to soak in this for twenty or thirty minutes so that your hands will soften," she told him, indicating the container she was working on.

"I'm aware of all the benefits of a paraffin bath," he said. His voice came from behind, low and steady, man deep, flowing over and around her.

For one fleeting second, Faith had a vision of what it would be like to be a patient, to have to lie still beneath Nathan's gaze while he conducted an examination. The thought made her squirm so much she nearly dropped the paraffin she was holding. And it made her angry. With herself. Hadn't she had to assure countless male patients that therapy was purely "clinical," that they should not be embarrassed, that they should think of her in the same light they would a doctor conducting a medical examination?

And here she was, entertaining lewd thoughts about Nathan Murphy just because he had a deadly set of eyes and a voice that made her nerves go on red alert.

She plunked the paraffin into the container to heat it. Struggling for something to say, she grasped the first thought that entered her head. "I've never worked with someone of your ilk before, someone in the medical profession. It's a bit—"

"Annoying?" he asked, sounding tremendously pleased.

"That's too mild a term," she admitted, waving one hand in the air. "Look, doctor, I've worked with high-powered executives, members of the clergy, lots of people who radiate authority, and it's never fazed me one bit. But a doctor, that could be a problem. Only one of us can be in charge, because therapy is a delicate blending of caring and control, just like surgery, I'd imagine. If you try to run the show, if we cross swords, you could really hurt yourself, do irreparable damage."

She turned, looking him full in the face, and saw the rebellious light in his eyes. "And don't," she warned, "don't you dare say that your hands are irreparably damaged already, because if you're the doctor that they say you are, you know that's not true. You've neglected treatment that should have been started a long time ago, and that's definitely going to slow things down. But with the proper treatment, the proper care, you'll operate again. On the other hand, if you second-guess me, if you try to pull rank and threaten your chances for recovery in any way, I—well, who knows? I just might lose it and wring your neck. Then we'll both be in trouble. You see the problem?"

Her hands were bunched into fists and she was leaning toward him when she realized that he was looking at her from beneath raised brows.

"Are you always this intense about your work, Ms. Reynolds, or is it just me who lights your fuse?"

Faith opened her mouth to speak, but not knowing what to say, she quickly closed it again. She hadn't meant to let him get to her like that. And while it was a fact that she did tend to be dedicated to her work, she wasn't usually given to making such impassioned speeches. Or even such threatening ones. The fact that she'd let him see that he irritated her both flustered and embarrassed her.

Turning, she quickly finished what she was doing and prepared to begin. This was just a job, she reminded herself again. Nathan Murphy was just a patient, like any other.

But then she felt him close behind her. She hadn't heard him moving, but she felt his presence, knew that he was there.

"Any other words of wisdom you'd like to drop on me, Ms. Reynolds?" he asked, his low, slightly gritty voice seeping into her senses once again.

"Yes," she said, testing the temperature of the melting paraffin. Now was as good a time as any to speak her mind. She'd already made her position on his rank clear. She might as well go the extra mile. "I'd like to drop all the formalities. I'm used to being on a first name basis with my patients, and a title definitely gets in the way. Therapy, like it or not, is a very personal kind of relationship. If I have to bow and scrape, things are definitely going to stall somewhere down the line."

Turning completely around, Faith looked up at him. Amazingly enough, he didn't even sneer at that "bow and scrape" line. Both of them knew that if she'd been wearing horns and a tail, she couldn't have looked more perturbed or less deferential. Instead, he simply nodded.

"If you and I are going to go head-to-head, it'll be easier to lay into each other if we're on a first name basis...Faith."

Immediately, Faith recognized her error. Her name sounded so intimate on his lips, like a touch instead of a word. But there was no going back now. Soon enough he'd be calling her names that didn't sound nearly so alluring. Therapy could, at times, be painful.

"Well, then, Nathan, I'll just finish up here, and we'll get started," she said, trying his name on her lips. She felt as if she'd just said something erotic, forbidden, and hastily she repeated it to herself several times. *Nathan. Nathan. Nathan.* In time, it would become easy, ordinary, she was sure. Just like all her other patients. It had to.

But when the time came to actually get Nathan to sit down and begin at last, he simply stared at her when she motioned him to the table where they'd be working.

"Give me one good reason why I should sit down and do as you ask," he said.

"I'll do better than that, I'll give you two. First of all, I happen to know that Dr. Anderson is holding something over your head or you wouldn't have even let me in the door. And then, of course, there's the fact that if you don't sit down right now and let me get to this, I'll have to call my son's sitter and tell her to run a pair of pajamas over here for me, after all. I'm prepared to sit here all night if need be. You'll just have to put up with me longer if you fight me."

His brow had raised when she'd divulged the fact that she knew about Anderson's ultimatum. Now he stood there, silent, his jaw set, hard, as he watched her. Finally, he took a step in her direction. He held out his hands as if he'd like to do something with them, something unpleasant, if only he could.

"Staying the night, that wouldn't be very fair to your kid, would it?" His voice was deceptively quiet. Anyone else with a deathly look like that in their eyes would have been shouting.

"No, Nathan, it wouldn't be very fair at all," she admitted, meeting his stare. "Not fair to Cory or to me. We miss each other when we're apart. But what would that matter to you, anyway? You've got your own agenda."

When Faith mentioned Cory's name, she almost thought she saw Nathan flinch. Inwardly she chided herself. Having heard a little of Nathan's history, knowing what he'd told her about children and family, she knew that he was suffering over the loss of his own child. Using Cory's name, making this personal in order to get what she wanted was a low blow, hitting below the belt. But just as she was about to open her mouth to apologize, Nathan dropped into the chair. He slid his hands across the table.

"Hell, I only have one bed, lady," he said by way of explanation. "And you'd probably hog the sheets."

"Believe me, Nathan," Faith said, placing his right hand in the paraffin bath, "if I ever find myself having to spend the night here, who's hogging the sheets will be the least of your worries. I wouldn't forgive you easily for forcing my hand."

"Or hurting your child," he said roughly.

Faith stopped what she was doing, looked at him. "I shouldn't have brought Cory into the conversation."

But, of course, she hadn't brought her son into the conversation. Nathan had. As if he just realized that fact, Nathan turned away, looking down at his hands.

"How long did you say this was for?" he asked, as though he'd just discovered a newfound interest in the therapy he'd been fighting a few minutes earlier.

"Not much longer," she assured him. "We'll start slow and easy."

But as she began to work with Nathan, Faith realized that dealing with this man would probably never be easy—or ordinary. She'd always been able to establish a certain amount of camaraderie with her patients while maintaining a professional distance.

Usually Faith was so keyed in on the tasks that she lost track of her surroundings. But that wasn't the case with Nathan. As she talked him through the first moves, began to flex fingers that no longer functioned properly and that surely hurt, Faith was very aware, not just of his hands and his reactions to the now unfamiliar movement, but also to the rest of him.

Sitting across from her at the table, he still seemed close, as if she could feel the heat emanating from him. The afternoon sun was bright and the wide berth of windows that fronted the house reached from floor to ceiling, but his shoulders were broad enough to block a good share of the light.

As always, Faith was alert to any indication that her patient was tiring, that he needed to rest.

"You don't have to watch yourself around me," she said. "It's no secret that your fingers have lost a great deal of their flexibility. Don't worry about groaning or letting me know if this is hurting."

"You want me to sit here and whine?" he asked, but his words were uttered through slightly clenched teeth.

"I want you to let me know what you're feeling."

He stopped cold then, his hands freezing within her own. "Forget it, Faith," he said, staring her down. "Spilling my guts is off-limits. And I don't care what you threaten me with."

At that, Faith blew out a breath. She smoothed her hand over the back of his where it lay flat on the table. "I'm not asking you to tell me things that are none of my business. But I am here to help you, Nathan, like it or not," she said, one long strand of her hair falling forward as she leaned closer to snag his attention. "You have to at least be a little honest with me. It's important that I know when you're tiring. Otherwise, I'll be doing more harm than good."

When Nathan leaned over to answer her, his lips were so close that she could feel the warmth of his breath. He'd slid his hands across the table so that his fingertips were perilously close to her body.

"This is your show, Faith," he said clearly, distinctly. "You've gotten your way so far. But asking me to act like a child wasn't part of the deal."

"I wasn't," she whispered. "I wouldn't." Heaven only knew that with his hands mere inches below the line where her breasts extended over the table, Faith was incapable of thinking of him as anything but a man. And she was angry with herself.

This wasn't supposed to happen. This never happened. Allowing herself to think of Nathan as anything but a patient was totally unwise, both as a therapist and as a woman.

"I think we should take a breather," she managed to get out. "You need a rest and so do I."

She could tell by the set line of his jaw that he thought she was babying him, that she didn't really need a rest, but he would have been wrong. She did need a rest, at least a few minutes to compose herself and get her thoughts back on the right course, back to Nathan's condition and away from the man.

"I'm a very honest person, Nathan," she said, as though he had voiced the question. "I'm just asking you to be honest with me, too."

He stared at her for long seconds. She knew he was weighing her words, doing a reality check, wondering if she was, in fact, being honest or whether she was simply trying to manipulate him. His concerns were valid. She hated condescension herself, had occasionally seen people in her profession use methods that stole their patients' dignity. It was rare, but it did occur.

Finally, he shook his head. "All right, then. There's some discomfort, but no unbearable pain."

It wasn't exactly the answer she wanted. Unbearable was a relative term. Still, she knew it was all she would get from him today. She would have to be satisfied with what little he had given her.

"We've been at it a long time," she said. "I'll get us something to drink, if you don't mind."

His outstretched hand stopped her. "No. That wasn't part of the deal. We work and then you leave."

Faith let out a deep breath of frustration. "Were you always this big a jerk, or is this a recent addition to your personality? Nathan, we've been here awhile. I hardly think a drink of water is going to make a big difference in time."

And without waiting for him to concur, she marched toward the back of the house in what she assumed was the general vicinity of the kitchen.

Nathan was right behind her, dogging her footsteps so he was there when she stepped into the shadowy kitchen and came upon the mess. Dishes were everywhere, none of them clean. The floor was strewn with crumbs and bits of food. The place looked like an explosion had gone off, littering every available surface.

The words *Oh my gosh* came to mind, but Faith never let them leave her lips. Nathan had known what she would find. He hadn't wanted her here.

Taking a breath, she picked her way across the floor gathering up dishes as she went, making her way to the sink. Behind her all was silent, the only sound in the room that of glass dragging against stoneware.

Faith felt a sliver of glass scrape her thumb as she reached into the sink to close the drain. She bit down on her lip, folded her thumb into her fist. Turning slowly, she faced him.

He was looking away.

"We'll get someone in here right away, Nathan. I know a woman who cooks and cleans. She's very good, very reasonable, and she needs the work."

"I had someone here, but she quit. Besides, I've told Dan that I don't want anyone hanging around."

"And he let you get away with it? I'm beginning to have less respect for the man than I once did. If it wasn't his urging that brought me here, I think I might have a talk with him. As it is, and given your resistance to everything I've tried to do for you, I guess I might understand. Like I said, I'll call someone."

"And I said—"

"Please." Faith held up one hand. "Don't say it. I know you want to be left alone. But given the status of this kitchen, I find it surprising that you don't already have plenty of company. In the form of midnight visitors—six legged ones. For the last time, Murphy, don't argue with me. You don't want me to bring out the heavy artillery again, do you? I'm not leaving here tonight—"

His cough was sudden and unexpected. It stalled her in midsentence. But when she stepped toward him, he seemed to have nothing wrong with his throat.

"Don't bother finishing that last sentence if you're going to threaten me with a pajama party again, Faith. I've gotten the idea. You're ready to play camp out if I don't give in to your every whim, if I don't agree to your every demand. All right, damn it, call in the troops. Invite a woman to my house to cook and clean, invite a thousand. Right now I'm about ready to have the entire universe over if it will get *you* out of my hair."

In truth, Nathan thought, he was ready to have anyone in his home. Anyone but her. Because she was the one making him squirm. She was the one who smelled softly of lemon, whose long, honey-colored hair dangled over her shoulders and played peekaboo with gently curving breasts—breasts that had been within reach of a caress for the last hour. If his hands had been capable. If he had been willing.

Biting her lip, she was nodding, her eyes big and solemn. In spite of the tough-guy attitude she'd been wearing, he could see the vulnerability imprinted on her irises. She'd bluffed him time and time again. Or maybe she'd really meant what she'd said. He couldn't take that chance, wanted her out of here, out of his life as quickly as possible, her and her little boy whose name he hadn't wanted to know.

And he'd do whatever she said if it meant she would go. Soon.

As she stepped to the sink and turned on the water, she opened her hand and he saw the small trace of red. "You cut yourself."

"It's nothing."

"It's not nothing, and save the stupid, macho lines for me. I've got more practice," he said, moving to her side. He motioned for her to hold out her hand, then cursed himself for his inability to fix even this small nick that was weeping blood and had to be painful.

"Damn it, Faith, call the woman," he told her. "It's my fault there's broken glass in the first place. Call her. Tonight."

Faith took his outstretched, useless hand. "Don't worry, Nathan. I just need a bandage."

He knew his eyes must look like storm clouds. He felt stupid, useless. More useless than he had felt since the accident. "I don't even have a bandage," he growled.

The woman had the nerve to laugh. She actually laughed. He was angry and ashamed and she was laughing.

"It's not a hanging offense, Nathan. You probably have lots of company in the world. But it doesn't matter, anyway. I've got one. All mothers carry a large supply."

Leaving the room, she retrieved her purse, pulled out a neon green strip and wrapped it around her finger. "Cory's favorite color," she confided. "Come on, let's finish up your session while you're not arguing for once."

She was impossible, unbelievable. Any other woman would have left him alone and helpless hours ago. The way he'd snapped at her yesterday, she should have slapped him and slammed the door in his face on the way out. He wouldn't have blamed her. But she was smiling. Joking. Teasing. He wondered if she treated all her patients that way and felt a return of his former sour mood.

Grumpily he sat down and slipped his hands across the table. She took them in her own strong ones, bending and straightening his fingers, explaining the exercises he was to do on his own time, as if she were dealing with a normal, pleasant man.

His eyes lit on her naked wrist. "Where's your brace-let?" he asked.

She looked up, her eyes startled and wide as though he'd caught her by surprise. "My bracelet?" she asked, ringing her wrist with her thumb and forefinger. "Oh, I don't wear jewelry when I'm working. It gets in the way."

Nathan pushed his palms against the tabletop when she would have taken his hands in her own again.

"Does your kid know that? A kid gives his mother something, he'd be hurt if she didn't wear it, especially if it was just to placate a bear of a patient, one who keeps his mom away at night."

Faith stilled, desisting in her attempts to get him back to work. She slowly nodded. "Cory knows about my work and what it means, or as much as a four-year-old can comprehend. He knows about the bracelet, but I'll be wearing it again by the time I get home. And by tomorrow, there'll be something else. He's always making something new. A picture. A badge. Something. I keep them in a special place and he knows I do."

"Okay. Yeah." Nathan's voice was gruff. He pulled his hands in close to his body.

"Besides," she said softly, "Cory knows better than to be jealous of my patients. He knows that this is business and that he's the most important person in my world, the only person I need or want in my world, really."

Nathan wondered if her words were a warning to him, and if she'd had to give this speech before. "What's he think of your being gone at night?"

When she shrugged, her faint, lemon scent drifted to him. Her breasts kissed the thin cotton of her blouse. Nathan pushed his palms harder against the wood.

"I don't know yet," she said softly. "This is his first night without me. I imagine it will be an adjustment—for both of us. But . . . we'll get used to it. That's the way of things."

She reached out, but he didn't place his hands in her own.

"It's the first night, Faith. You've put me through my paces. Go home now. Go home to your boy."

Faith stared at him. He saw her lips thin with determination, knew what she was going to say. Closing his eyes, he passed one hand across his face, stifled a shudder at the thought of the little boy watching out the window for the woman who wasn't home yet.

"Go home, Faith," he said, more gently this time, trying to keep the grating edge out of his voice. "Please."

Ten seconds of silence. Then, "All right. You're right. We don't want to overdo things and risk overtiring your muscles on the first day."

Nathan stifled his sigh of relief, let the guilt wash away, the guilt that had been building ever since he'd thought of that boy making a gift for his mother and waiting impatiently for her return. He didn't want to think of four-year-old boys—or soft, silky women with sad blue green eyes.

Dragging the chair away from the table with a backward thrust of his body, Nathan rose as Faith busied herself putting things away, making sure things were ready for the next time.

"How long do you think it will be," he asked, "before we're done for good?"

She paused in her packing. "I'm not sure. That'll depend on you and your body's limitations, but I can assure you that we'll work as quickly as possible. We'll finish as soon as we can."

Nathan watched her as she went about her business. He didn't want to notice her, didn't want to note how slim and pretty she was. He didn't want to see the pale underside of her arm when her cropped sleeve slid high, or the way her white slacks cupped her bottom when she reached across the table to pick up something.

Sitting across from her today had been hell, and not just because of the physical pain of trying to work fingers that were used to lying stiff and still. Her lemon-scented hair made him want to lean closer, to move in and invade her space. And her skin... although the sensation in his fingers was still returning, the rest of his nerve endings were perfectly intact. Faith Reynolds had skin that was meant for nuzzling with lips and teeth and tongue. The urge to bend close, to breathe in the essence of her, had caught him by surprise, made him angry. With himself, not her. She seemed oblivious to her appeal, to the fact that she was like a sensual magnet, calling up needs he'd pushed out of his life long ago. Needs he wasn't going to tend to no matter what the provocation.

And when she'd spoken of her son—damn, he wasn't going to think about this. This was day one of something that might go on for a very long time. He couldn't afford to think this way, he damn well wasn't going to allow himself another thought of her, not one. Because thinking was all he would ever do anyway, and thinking about things that were off-limits, out of reach, he'd learned, could drive a man stark, raving crazy.

"Nathan?" She had planted herself in front of him, all five feet three inches. She was smiling up at him with that warm, wary expression. It was time to take a step back. Maybe more than one step.

"I guess I'll see you tomorrow," he said, striving for distance, at least in his voice.

"Tomorrow, Nathan." And reaching out, she placed her hand on the bare expanse of his forearm. Not his hand. She knew his grasp was still imperfect, that he would have trouble with a handshake. But his arm was still alive with nerves.

Her small hand was velvet soft, her fingertips cool as she pressed them to the heat of his exposed skin. Nathan's lungs stopped pumping air.

If he hadn't been so shocked at his reaction, he would have laughed. He'd just spent an hour in her company as she ran her hands over his own, again and again. Now, with her palm simply resting on his skin, he was wild with sensation.

And ashamed. The way she jerked away suddenly, the alarmed look in her eyes just before she moved out the door, he almost wondered if he hadn't said something, done more than he thought he had. At the very least, she'd surely felt the pounding of his pulse beneath her fingers.

Staring out the window long after she'd gone, Nathan cursed himself for a fool. At his age he should be capable of controlling himself better than that.

Especially when his reactions didn't mean anything, when he wasn't about to pay attention to them.

He'd had his chance at life, at happiness, at love, and he'd blown it, abominably; hurt his wife and his child, not been there when they needed him. He wasn't about to risk involvement of any kind, on any level. Not again.

And neither was Faith if he hadn't misunderstood her words.

Realizing that Faith had her own barbed wire fences made Nathan breathe a little easier. She wasn't interested in him. Not as a man, anyway.

That was fine. That was good.

He'd come face-to-face with temptation and battled it down. Everything would work out from here on. They'd get by with no more problems. He'd withstood the test of touch.

But in the dark of the night, in the midst of a dream, Nathan woke to the feel, the memory of long feminine fingers sliding against his skin, stroking his flesh.

And the memory was not of his Joanna; this was not his wife's touch. The knowledge seared his soul. Joanna. He had failed her in life, let his career get in the way of her needs. He's failed to protect her when it had mattered most. Now he'd even betrayed her in his dreams.

But now he was awake, Nathan realized, shunting aside the memories of Faith's innocent touch. Awake and very aware of the difference between reality and dreams. Reality was that Faith Reynolds was his therapist, and as such, he had to work with her, like it or not. Reality was knowing that one day she'd be no more than a woman, or rather a medical professional, in his past.

Nathan lay back, waiting for morning. All too soon Faith would return, and everything would start all over again. He should sleep, get some rest so that he'd be up to the challenge of dealing with her. But still he lay there, eyes open, watching for the dawn. He had no desire for sleep—or dreams—again tonight.

# Chapter Three

The next morning Faith woke, knowing she didn't want to face the bathroom mirror. She hadn't gotten enough sleep, her eyes were probably puffy, her hair hopelessly tangled from tossing and turning in her bed. All because she'd touched Nathan and been seared with a flame of pure, unadulterated sizzle. That tiny bit of contact, a mere brush of fingers against warm male flesh and her blood had heated, her vision had blurred, her lips had tingled. And she'd lost an entire night's rest.

Now she didn't even want to look at herself, but this was a work day. Time to face the music, hit the bathroom running, make breakfast, get dressed, tend to her child's needs.

And so, braving the mirror, Faith peered at herself, tentatively.

A groan escaped her.

"God, no."

The face that stared back at her was familiar. It was definitely hers. But this morning the expression in her eyes, that wistful, yearning look about her lips also bore vague similarities to her mother, Helen Reynolds. Just the thought was enough to make Faith pale.

Her mother had spent her life hungering after men who were all wrong for her, who didn't want her, men who'd broken her heart while Faith looked on. And Faith had promptly grown up and made the same mistake herself. With Jim, her ex-husband.

"Not again," she said, grasping the metal edge of the medicine cabinet and pulling it open, obliterating her reflection as she fumbled for the aspirin. "Never again."

The cycle was broken. She'd learned her lesson the hard way, and she would not be a fool again. She had no intention of mooning after a man she couldn't have just because he was virile and handsome and made her nerves do a tango whenever their skin happened to touch. She had no intention of doing anything connected with the words *emotions, feelings,* or *desires*.

She had her self-esteem to consider, that kernel of pride that was her lifesaver enabling her to hold her head high. More importantly, though, she had Cory to think of. Cory was her everything; he brought the sun into her life every day of her life. They were a family, inseparable. Yet the very word *family* had been censored from Nathan's life; it made his eyes turn dark and bleak. She'd seen it happen. He was not for her and Cory—in any fashion.

Faith took out her makeup, ventured another tentative peek into the glass. Good. The lecture had done her good. She was herself again, firm and in control. And she had a son to see to.

Two minutes later, she entered her son's room to find him struggling with his sock.

"Stupid sock," he grumbled. "Can't get it on."

"Because you've got it upside down, tiger. See?" Sliding the heel of the sock around to snugly fit Cory's small foot, Faith hugged him close and handed him his shirt.

"Can you manage the buttons?" she asked, allowing him to struggle for success on his own.

Cory gifted her with a frown when he finally got his head through the opening. "Mom, come on, I'm a big guy. Course I can." So Faith sat back, hoping she wouldn't be late while Cory fumbled both buttons closed at the neck.

Breakfast and twenty minutes had passed by the time they made it to the car, so Faith's mind was on the speed limit and the annoying red lights when out of the corner of her eye she caught Cory staring at her.

"Mom, what's that guy like? The one you see at night."

With a great deal of luck, Faith kept the car from wobbling. "You mean Dr. Murphy? I don't know. He's just a man, a man who needs my help."

"Why can't you help him during the day? Why do you have to be gone at night? Mandy grumbles for staying late, and she doesn't cook too good. She doesn't sing, either. And she can't help me with the list. I miss you, Mom."

Without thought, Faith took her foot off the accelerator, tapped the brakes. Slowing, she pulled the car over to the side of the road and turned to her son. "Cory, I miss you, too. So much. And I'm really sorry about the late hours," she told him, straightening the cap on his head. "But this is a special case, and it won't be for long. Not too long, anyway. We'll be back to our old life soon. I promise."

She ran the backs of her fingers over his cheek in a gentle caress. He was so beautiful and much too intense, this child of hers.

"'Cause he's a doctor? Is that why it's special?"

Faith shifted the car back into drive and took one last glance at Cory. "Partly," she agreed on a sigh. "That's part of it. The hospital wants him back."

Long seconds of silence ensued. They were nearly to Mandy's house when Cory spoke again. "Guess I don't like doctors much. You have that list with you?"

Pulling up in front of the baby-sitter's house, Faith turned to help Cory with his seat belt. "The Daddy List? No, it's at home."

He nodded and frowned. "Okay, but when you get home tonight, I want you to write something on it. All right, Mom?"

Tapping his nose with her finger, Faith smiled. She climbed from the car and moved to help him out. "You got it, sport. What is it you want me to write down?"

But in truth Faith already knew.

"Write down 'Not a doctor,'" he told her. "Okay?"

"Definitely okay," she promised as she dropped him at the door and kissed him goodbye.

*Not a doctor and black hair and brown eyes.* Faith felt a sense of calm wash over her, thinking of the way Cory's list was progressing. She couldn't have made a better list herself.

But darn, working in a hospital as she did, the choices were being pared down considerably. And with her hours so booked up, she had no time right now. None at all.

It was going to take longer than she'd hoped to find the right man for her and Cory.

Walking into Nathan's house was like tiptoeing over a land mine today. She had taken herself in hand for the touching incident yesterday, which made for a slightly uncomfortable atmosphere today. And Nathan himself seemed quiet, too quiet. Like the eerie absence of sound just before a storm rips up the sky. He'd stopped fighting her.

Maybe he had noted her reaction to him the day before. She didn't see how he could have missed it. Her hands were shaking so badly by the time she'd left that she had barely been able to get the door open.

The thought that she'd been so transparent was embarrassing. Faith promised herself to be nothing short of the perfect therapist today.

"Let's get to work, Nathan," she commanded, getting right down to business.

Silently he sat and pushed his hands toward her. "Let's get it over with," he agreed.

Faith noticed that he didn't look at her; it was as if they were two sets of hands, no bodies. Perhaps she really had done a poor job of hiding her reaction to him yesterday and he was uncomfortable with her.

Well, he wouldn't have to worry about it happening again. From now on, she would touch him only in a clinical capacity. She would notice nothing but his progress as a patient.

But as Faith leaned over Nathan, guiding him through a series of exercises, she couldn't help but be aware of her surroundings. When they stopped to give Nathan a chance to rest, she couldn't keep her eyes from roaming.

Nathan's house was all natural cedar and sunlight; a beautiful, airy house with few walls. It should have been homey, cozy. Instead it was somewhat...naked, empty. The furniture was warm, large and masculine, but the tables stood empty, their surfaces barren. The shelves in the room held little. There wasn't a plant in sight, and the walls—the walls were large, lonely expanses of shining white. No pictures, no plaques, no certificates or personal mementos.

Nothing except one small, framed portrait sitting on a distant shelf. A man, a woman, a child.

Faith recognized Nathan's face immediately, although the deep sense of satisfaction in his smile was foreign to her. He didn't look like that now. He no longer smiled, at least not that way.

The woman in the picture was lovely, with curling auburn hair and dark eyes. But the child was what drew Faith's attention, mesmerized her. She was small and beautiful, a picture postcard little girl, very much like her mother...except for the eyes like green jewels and the dimples that dented her cheeks. It was hard to believe that child was gone, that somewhere on this earth she wasn't smiling still, waiting for her father to come and find her.

Faith turned and looked at Nathan, at the sharp jawline turned from her, and she saw that his gaze had followed her own. He was staring at the picture as though he hadn't known it was there, as if he hadn't seen it in a long time and was wishing that he hadn't seen it now.

Finally with a jerk, he turned his head away, looked straight into her own eyes which she knew were laced with concern. He held out his hands once again.

"More," he said, nudging his fingers against her own. "I'm ready to begin again."

Faith reached out, took his hands. It was all she could do since she knew he wouldn't welcome her comments or her questions about his family.

As she made sure that his hands were relaxed, she couldn't help noting how small and feminine her fingers looked against his. And yet her helpless-looking hands were still capable while his grip was still slack, his fingers clumsy. The accident had taken so much. He'd lost it all. His family, his skills.

Resolutely, Faith sat up higher, more determined. This impairment to his hands wasn't permanent. They could do something about it. And Nathan was impatient to do just that, or at least to work himself free of her presence. She could tell by the way he sat forward, trying to begin before she was done examining him.

"We'll get there, Nathan. I won't let you down. But you have to let me set the pace. I'm trained to know what's too much, when to move ahead and when to slow down."

Nathan suddenly flipped his hands over so that her fingers were resting on his scarred palms, more evidence that for once *he* was the patient.

Slowly he lowered their hands to the table. "I'm trying to step all over you again. One more example of just how annoying and pushy we doctors can be?"

"You sound like my son," Faith said with a laugh. Then realizing her error, she promptly sucked in her lips.

Nathan tilted his head. "Cory have a bit of a bad experience with doctors, did he?"

"Oh no, nothing like that," she said, then stopped, unsure what to say. "It's just . . . it's just—nothing."

Nathan held one injured hand out as if waiting for her to put something in it or asking for her to come clean. "It's not nothing judging by the look on your face," he told her. "There's a problem with your boy?"

"Nothing much," she said, reaching for the hands that he now moved away from her touch. "You were right yesterday. Cory's just having a little trouble adjusting to my being away. It'll get better."

A frown appeared on Nathan's face. "He's only four, I think you said. Young."

She nodded. "Really, Nathan, I'm sorry I mentioned it. I'm sorry I even mentioned Cory. It was a slip. Let's get back to your therapy."

Reluctantly, it seemed, Nathan moved back into position.

Five minutes later, he looked up. "I asked you not to bring him, but don't apologize just for saying his name, Faith. You're his mother, damn it. Of course you're going to think of him. He's your child. He's your world. That's the way of things."

But when Faith opened her mouth to speak, Nathan's face was shuttered, closed again. And in the days that followed she noticed that the picture on the shelf was gone. Now the room was totally bare... and Nathan was more distant than ever.

The days went by, and in a short time, Faith and Nathan fell into a pattern, a sort of wary, impersonal waltz as she moved him through a series of exercises, taught him what to do when she was away, kept a careful watch on his progress.

She never touched him again, except for his hands. She never mentioned Cory, never asked any personal questions, tried to avoid those mesmerizing eyes as she moved through the motions of helping Nathan regain the flexibility in his fingers.

He was a good patient, intelligent, driven. But she could sense that he was growing more impatient as time went on. She could feel the lava starting to boil beneath the surface.

One day she came in and found him staring at the small bit of rubber that he squeezed to strengthen his grip.

Looking up as if she'd startled him, Nathan managed a small and sheepish smile. "I'm beginning to hate the sight of red rubber," he confided.

She raised one brow and smiled back. "I could get you blue."

He stood then, forcing her to look up at him. With one finger he reached out and touched her still smiling mouth. A small feather of skin against skin, but Faith's lips burned as though he'd stroked her with flame.

"Don't bother," he said, withdrawing his hand with a small frown. "I'll survive. You look—you look different today. Happier. Are things . . . all right at home?"

It was the first time he'd referred to the conversation they'd had about Cory. And Faith didn't fail to notice that his question was rather nonspecific.

"Fine," she said with a nod. "I see your grip's improving a bit," she added, nodding toward his hand, moving the conversation onto safer ground.

They were back to their professional relationship. It was as if they'd never smiled, as if Nathan's touch had gone unnoticed. Faith should have been glad, she was the one who had made the choice to ignore his concern, his contact, and keep things businesslike. But as the evening passed, she found herself wishing she could make him smile again, a real smile this time, full lipped and devastating. Dangerous.

There was a good reason for wanting his smiles, she told herself, a very good reason. Recovery involved more than muscles and bone. It was as much psychological as physical. And she'd been cheating Nathan so far, trying to protect herself at his expense. She'd try to remember that in the future.

And the future came sooner than she expected. She was reminded again of just how all-encompassing a therapist's job was a few days later when a hospital staff meeting threw Faith's schedule out of whack. She arrived at Nathan's early to find Hannah, Nathan's new housekeeper, still there.

"Just leaving," she said. "I'm out tonight," the woman boomed at her. Hannah had a body like a semi and a voice to match. "Got a family dinner, but don't worry. I've got Mr. Nathan all set up. The food's all set to go. I'll be back in the morning bright and early."

"But where's Nathan?" Faith asked, looking around.

"Oh, he's about. In the shower," Hannah said, cocking her head.

"Nathan? In the shower? Alone?" Faith asked.

"Alone? Well, I should think so," Hannah told her with a bewildered look. "Might as well sit down. I ran out of liquid soap and he wouldn't let me buy anymore. Wants to stop babying himself, he says, even though managing a bar of soap's a little rough. Takes him a bit of time to get anywhere near clean. But he's a very independent man. All male, you know. Doesn't like having anyone make things easier for him. Likes to manage alone."

Faith certainly did know. She remembered her first glimpse of the kitchen. Before Hannah had come. That's how well he had managed alone.

And as Hannah bustled out to her car, Faith wondered just how Nathan was faring. He'd been so tense lately. He needed successes, not the frustration of handling a slippery bar of soap. She wanted his attempts at doing things for himself to offer encouragement, give him a sense of accomplishment. The prospect of Nathan wrestling a slithery piece of soap across his body wasn't exactly what she had in mind. And Faith knew then that she *had* been lax, that she should have discussed such things with him, made sure that he didn't need help beyond what Hannah could give him.

What kind of a therapist was she, she asked herself. The answer came back, fast and hard. She was a damned good therapist, one who was just a bit off-kilter at times with this particular patient.

Faith stood outside the door of the bathroom, shifting from foot to foot. Eight times she heard the bar drop, heard Nathan curse loudly as she stood there, wrapping her arms tightly about herself, clenching her elbows.

She nearly called out his name, but forced herself to remain quiet. If he wanted help, he would say so.

Still, the whole process seemed interminable. What time had it been when he walked into that bathroom? How long had he been in there? Was that the soap dropping she heard again?

No, it had to be him putting it down for the final time. The water stopped. He must be getting dried off.

The thought of the whole length of Nathan naked and wet as he pushed the towel over his skin was too much for Faith. She couldn't just stand here anymore. She especially didn't want to be found hovering outside the door when he emerged.

Moving into the kitchen, she tried to prepare herself for his reaction to finding her there. He'd know that she'd heard his struggle with the shower. How was he going to feel about that? She could guess that he wouldn't be pleased.

No matter. Her job was to be encouraging, remind him that his strength was returning slowly, that things would get better.

But as she turned at the sound of him nearing the doorway, she couldn't think of a single word of advice to offer. He was standing there in unbuttoned jeans, his shirt opened all the way, barefoot and still damp in places. His hair was wet and spiky, his eyes mirrored his frustration at the less than satisfying experience he'd just gone through.

Still, he wasn't going to say anything. She could see it in the belligerent set of his chin, the way he was looking at her, daring her to offer any of those inadequate comments she'd been about to make.

Instead, she simply turned and took two glasses from the cabinet, pouring the tea she'd found in the fridge. At the last moment she remembered that she'd poured Nathan's glass too full. He would have trouble handling it.

"Leave it," he said. "I'll manage."

With a movement that seemed like a slow-motion video, Nathan slid his hand to the glass, resting it there a moment. Then, slowly, he curled one finger around the curved surface. Then another, and another, until his hand was securely around the perimeter of the glass.

Gritting his teeth, he slowly raised the container to his mouth, his knuckles white, his brow furrowed.

After three deep swallows, Nathan clattered the glass to the counter, turning to her defiantly. "You look just like my mother used to when I climbed up to get the cat off the roof. I warn you, if you say 'Very good, Nathan,' I'll smash this glass against the wall."

She hadn't been planning to say that, but the words she'd been going to utter sounded equally condescending to her now. And she wasn't about to let him know that.

Instead, Faith looked him dead in the eye and filled his glass again. "You shatter that glass, and you'll take the broom and sweep up every broken bit."

They stood there, staring at each other, breathing heavily, their brows furrowed like two animals fighting for territory.

Then Nathan smiled, slow and lazy.

"You're a real lion tamer, Faith. One tough lady."

That's exactly the way she felt, like a shaky lion tamer caged up with an unpredictable and exhilarating beast. He was wild, he was dangerous, and she didn't know what the hell to do with him except try to keep him from getting too close to her—or hurting himself.

Faith needed to back away. She couldn't think and look into Nathan's eyes at the same time. Dropping her gaze, she found herself staring at his exposed chest, the light, silky hair that covered it.

"Buttons are still a problem," he said, as if reading her mind.

It was a difficult admission to make, she was sure.

"I can handle a few buttons," she offered. She'd spoken quickly, not wanting him to have to listen to the silence, wondering if she was pitying him. Now, seeing the sudden fire that came to life in Nathan's eyes, Faith wondered who was actually to be pitied here.

"It's all right, Faith. I'd say that dressing me goes beyond the bounds of duty."

It was also beyond the bounds of what Faith felt she'd be comfortable doing right now, but she'd promised herself to become more involved in Nathan's progress, to stop shying away from him like a fresh-faced teenager faced with her idol.

"I've dressed patients before," she said, and it was the truth. But those other patients had been nothing like Nathan.

At her words his look turned dark, intense.

She moved to him, lifted her hands to tug on the edges of his shirt—and instantly felt warm, hair-roughened skin. Damp flesh pulsing beneath her fingertips. She inhaled and breathed in his scent—soap...man. Nathan. Beneath the pads of her fingertips, she could feel his heart beating, or it seemed that way. Her fingers stilled. She looked up at him, uncertain how to go on.

"Maybe it would be better to leave your shirt unfastened," she faltered. "You're still damp." Swift heat flooded throughout her. "And it *is* warm in here."

"Maybe you're right," he said thickly.

But as Faith stepped back, she wasn't so sure. She could have had the buttons done up in a trice, and looking at the exposed muscles of Nathan's chest was almost as unnerving as touching him.

"Hannah left your dinner," she said quickly, looking for a change of subject.

Nathan let out a breath as if he, too, had been uncomfortable with their situation. He looked at the table, then turned back to Faith. "Care to join me? I'm starved. And frankly, I—I wouldn't mind the company."

What could she do when he asked so nicely? Nice for Nathan, at any rate. Managing a smile, Faith nodded. "Sounds good. Hannah left a meal big enough to feed the entire hospital."

Nathan watched her as she walked across the room to where Hannah had left the food. He was relieved to have her move away from him, and yet he felt a vague sense of loss at her going.

Thank God she'd given up on helping him with his shirt. When her strong, capable fingers had rested on his chest seconds earlier, he'd been afraid that he'd give in to the urge to touch her, too; to slide one hand beneath all that long, honey brown hair he'd been staring at for so long and expose the vulnerable nape of her neck. To his eyes. His lips.

He watched Faith as she arranged food on the plates, slicing the too-thick pieces of ham that Hannah had left, rearranging dishes, swaying as she worked. She was so petite, and yet so graceful. Her hands were delicate, gentle, he knew. She reached out and slid one finger over a plate and Nathan felt his mouth go dry. His mind made the leap.

Thoughts of that one slender finger sliding down his chest filled Nathan's consciousness.

Angrily, he pushed the picture away, and tried to envision his Joanna.

He took four deep breaths, and felt himself relaxing a bit. Faith was helping him by getting his dinner, something that wasn't in her job description. He should be helping her and instead he was—no, he wasn't going back down that path, not even to berate himself.

Pulling open a drawer, he clattered silverware about, biting down as he clutched up two forks, spoons and knives. He slammed the drawer shut, grasped the pull on a cabinet and grabbed two napkins, crushing them into his other hand.

"Nathan!"

Faith's cry made the skin tingle all the way down his back. The damn knife. She must have cut herself while she was helping him.

Whirling, he turned to her. But she didn't have a knife in her hand, she held nothing.

She was staring at him, a bright smile on her lips, a glistening teardrop rolling down her cheek.

"Faith? Faith, are you all right? What's wrong?"

In a second he was at her side. He dropped the silverware and napkins on the table and caught up her hands, bringing them closer to see if she'd hurt herself in some way.

She shook her head urgently, another tear making its way down her cheek.

With one finger, he traced the wet trail down her skin.

"Nathan, your hands," she whispered, staring at the hand that still held her own.

Instantly, he clutched her fingers tighter.

"You're holding things, you're gripping things. In fact, you've got my hand so tightly that I think my own fingers might break."

She was smiling like a rainbow turned upside down. Her tears were coming hard and fast, and Nathan realized that she was right. He loosened his grip immediately, but he didn't let go.

Instead he smiled back. "Did I hurt you?"

Faith shook her head. "Not really. Nathan, this is wonderful. I've been watching your progress for days now, and you *do* grip things, but only when you're concentrating, only with great effort. This is different, you did this without thinking, you did it naturally."

She was right. He'd been doing his damnedest *not* to think, to get her out of his mind. And now she was staring at him as if he were a gladiator, or a knight. As if he'd held hostile armies at bay for her instead of picking up a fork.

For the first time in ages, Nathan felt like a man, like a man who was going to be whole, physically at least. He'd said he hadn't wanted it, didn't care, and he hadn't. Not then. But now exhilaration poured through his body, ran through his veins like warm, healing water.

"Thank you, Faith," he said.

And without thought, he moved closer, slid his palms beneath her hair, brought his lips to hers.

She was so small that he had to bend slightly to reach her lips, and that, too, was enough to make him feel large and powerful and protective.

Slowly he brushed his lips back and forth across her own, savoring the feel of her, the sense of wholeness that he was feeling.

He felt her move closer, felt her hands climb to his temples, slip down to his neck. He knew the minute her lips pressed back against his own.

A groan escaped Nathan and he gathered her closer, lifting her off the ground and into his arms. She was so small and sweet and the curves of her breasts against his chest made him want to sink into her, lay her down here and now, kiss his way down her throat, down her belly.

His head was spinning. Her lips were like damp rose petals, soft and fragrant and pliant. Heady stuff. He wanted her now, her soft hips naked beneath him on crisp, tangled sheets. He wanted her willing and wanton, her long slender legs parting in invitation.

He nudged open her lips, raked her tongue with his own, sipping at her, losing himself in her. Sweet release.

"Faith, you're so warm, so giving. The feel of you—I want to—" His own words sounded in his head.

Faith's moan, her body moving against his stopped Nathan cold.

What in hell did he think he was doing? He had seen the tears on her face, knew that this was an emotional moment for her, for both of them. They'd both worked too damn hard, had too much pent-up emotion.

He shouldn't even be touching this woman, much less contemplating the things he'd been thinking of only seconds earlier.

"Faith," he groaned, his arms iron bands that pushed her away from him. "God, I'm sorry," he said, stepping back, turning away. "I'm so damn sorry."

Long seconds of silence stretched out, but he didn't turn to look at her, couldn't stand to see the disgust written on her face. Couldn't stand to think of his own betrayal. He'd wanted her. Needed her warmth. More than he could remember wanting, or needing, in years. Many years, not just the last two. The thought made him sick. Joanna had deserved better. And Faith...

"Don't worry," she said faintly, at last.

Her words finally made him turn to her. She sounded so small, so lost.

Her hair was falling around her face in soft, wanton waves that kissed her cheeks as she shook her head.

Nathan closed his eyes.

"Don't worry, Nathan. It's gratitude. It happens all the time," she assured him. "We were both carried away by the excitement of the moment. That's all."

*It happens all the time.* My God, did she mean that? Did men maul her at every turn, was that what she had to put up with? The thought of Faith fending off the advances of every grateful male she'd aided made Nathan's vision blur with anger. And most of it was directed dead center at himself.

"As I said, I'm sorry, Faith. At least accept my apology."

Faith looked at Nathan's angered eyes, passionate, stormy and so dark they were nearly black.

She opened her mouth to speak, but at his grim expression, she simply nodded.

"You should eat," she said, turning to the table.

"No."

She looked over her shoulder and saw the hand he'd held up to halt her progress. Slowly he returned his hand to his side, curled his fingers into the beginnings of a fist.

"You probably need to get home," he said.

It was exactly what she wanted to do. The memory of how she'd totally lost control in Nathan's arms only seconds ago, of how she'd practically been clinging to him, moving against him, filled her with shame. She wanted to run.

Faith took a deep breath.

"I'm not leaving until we're done with your session," she told him. "You've made progress, but there's still a lot of work ahead. You're a surgeon, your fine motor skills have to be perfect. So, let's go.''

He didn't argue, he didn't talk. He worked and he worked hard, but Faith had all she could do just to sit in the chair and make it through until it was time to go home.

When she finally made it to the door, Nathan was there before her, clutching the knob, swirling his thumb over the bright brass.

She almost managed a smile.

Beside her, Nathan blew out a long breath of air.

"Faith?"

"I'll be back tomorrow. And Nathan, please don't dwell on—on the kiss. Like I said, these things happen. It'll be best if we both forget it."

*These things happen. These things happen.* The words whirled and danced through her brain all the way home. *It's gratitude. These things happen.*

The only problem was that these things didn't happen. Not to her.

She'd let the moment get away from her at a time when Nathan was vulnerable, able to use his hands in new ways for the first time since the accident. He'd been swept away, it was natural. But she was the therapist. She was supposed to control the situation.

"Gratitude," she said with a moan. She couldn't believe how she'd thrown that word up to him, as though it would save her from the naked truth.

For the truth was that gratitude and such infatuations were not all that uncommon in therapist-patient relationships. But there was one sticking point here. The gratitude and infatuation was supposed to be on the part of the patient, not the therapist.

She had been right from the start. Nathan Murphy was dangerous.

The man had kissed her! Worse, she had kissed him back.

It would be an absolute miracle if she got any sleep at all tonight.

Hours later, as she lay wide-eyed and restless, silently waiting for the dawn to deliver her from her misery, Faith heard her son's first weak cry. She rose and went to him, but by morning it was clear. Cory was sick, dreadfully sick with the flu.

Faith was going to have to find someone to take her place with her patients today. Wearily she picked up the phone and began to dial.

# Chapter Four

The sound of Faith's voice on the other end of the line sent a frisson of heat coursing through Nathan's body. Unwelcome heat. He'd been trying not to think of her all day, didn't want to remember the feel of her softness pressed to the hard length of him or to wonder if she was working with other "grateful" patients today, if she'd been upset with herself for responding to him the night before. But no, she'd told him it was best to forget what had happened. And she was right. That's why he'd dusted off the picture of Joanna and Amy, put it back on the shelf this morning. As a reminder of what was important. As punishment.

"Nathan?" she asked when he didn't answer right away.

"I'm here," he assured her. "Is something wrong? Why are you calling?" His voice was gruffer than he had intended. Long seconds ticked by.

Maybe she was calling to say she'd had enough of him.

Maybe she was backing out the door the way he'd dared her to just a short time ago. Getting smart at last.

"Nathan, I'm calling because I—well, I can't be there tonight. My son—Cory's sick. The flu. I don't want to leave him, and besides, his baby-sitter has little ones, too. It wouldn't be right to expose her or to ask her to care for a sick child. But don't worry. I've found other therapists to fill in for me all day. I just wanted to let you know some-one else would be coming by."

So Faith *was* finally getting smart, leaving him behind.

Nathan looked across the room at the likeness of Joanna, forced himself to face the woman who represented all his failures, the woman who'd be laughing right now if she could. He'd always been the one canceling out on his wife, had been such a poor excuse for a husband. Her silent cen-sure had told him so, every time he'd been called away to the hospital, leaving her alone. She'd never been able to count on him, not even to protect her. And he'd hurt her, knew that he had. He hadn't deserved her.

He didn't deserve Faith, either. Silken-haired Faith with her tough-as-nails stance. Faith, with eyes like frosty blue icicles when her back was to the wall, that turned butter soft when she thought no one was looking, that melted com-pletely when a man held her close and quenched his thirst with her lips. No, he didn't deserve Faith Reynolds. He should never have taken advantage of her, shouldn't have rubbed away at her veneer and exposed the woman be-neath, the one who could be hurt by a man like him. But no matter... because now he didn't have to worry about that. She was withdrawing as his therapist. That was what this was all about, what she was trying to tell him.

She was clearing out, giving up on him, backing off. That was, after all, what he wanted, wasn't it? Hadn't he told her all along that he didn't want her around? Absolutely. So why—why in hell—did he feel so angry? Why did he suddenly feel like a frustrated volcano?

"Nathan," she said, breaking into his thoughts. "Listen. The woman who's coming is named Penny Damen. She'll be there—"

"No. No one's coming. Don't send her." Nathan's voice was low, hard. "My door's closed. And anyway, I'm surprised at you, Faith—wouldn't have thought anything could make you run. Not even me. If that's what this is about, then you don't need to worry. I won't touch you again. Call off your other therapist. I'll keep my gratitude to myself from now on. You can depend on it."

Full silence greeted Nathan's speech. It dragged out over the telephone wires, hung in the air as he waited. Four seconds. Five. Then, "You think I'm canceling on you because of yesterday? You think I'd back away just because a man, because a patient—"

"Slipped his tongue between your lips? Nipped your throat with his teeth? It's not exactly standard therapy procedure, Faith. And while I may be surprised, I certainly wouldn't blame you for walking away."

He could almost see her chest heaving, her blue green eyes flashing emerald sparks.

"Well, I would blame me, Nathan. What kind of therapist do you think I am? One who blows away in a breeze, one who bolts every time something unexpected comes up?

He wanted to laugh at that. Leave it to Faith to term a male patient wrapping his body around hers "something unexpected." Well, he supposed it was. Just as he supposed she was right. Remembering the way she'd stormed his fortress, pushed her way into his life against all his objections and threats, he couldn't imagine her turning tail and running now. Even though he *wouldn't* blame her. Even though she should. She sure as hell should.

"All right," he finally said. "You're no coward. I'll give you that, and nobody knows that better than me. So just put the dagger away, Faith. You win. I believe you, your son is sick. You can't be here, but...it doesn't matter, anyway. The reasons don't matter. Just don't send the other therapist. Don't send her. I'll wait this out till—"

Damn. Her reasons, real reasons for backing away finally hit him. Nathan let out a sigh, forked his fingers back through his hair, tried not to look at the picture of his daughter smiling as though happiness could never possibly die—as though children could never be hurt.

"I'm sorry, Faith," he suddenly said. "How *is* your boy, anyway? It's tough being so sick when you're a kid." He remembered. He *did* remember that, like it or not.

"He's, I don't know..." Faith's voice was low, hesitant. "Miserable. Quiet. Too quiet for Cory, but he'll be all right. In a few days, the doctor says. In the meantime, Nathan...Nathan, you can't wait. I'm sending a substitute. That's final."

He wanted to crunch the phone in his hands, crawl through the wires and stand in front of her, lean into her to get his point across. "I told you, Faith, that I didn't want to be gawked at. You and Anderson are just about all I can take. And you know what a jerk I can be, how uncooperative I am. Do you really want to ask this woman to put up with me knowing what she's walking into?"

"You want the truth? No, I don't. If someone's going to have to take grief from you, then I'd rather it was me. I'm used to it, at least. And it's very difficult asking someone to do a favor for me, knowing that I'm asking them to walk into an unpleasant situation. But Nathan, that's the way it has to be. This therapy—we're not talking about someone who merely needs to be able to pick up things and grasp them with a reasonable amount of strength. You know that, all too well. Your fingers have to be more than merely flexible, you have to have above average dexterity. Otherwise, during surgery, if your hands didn't cooperate, you could slip, maim someone—or at least be incapable of carrying out the tasks you'd want to do. These sessions aren't just mildly amusing activities we take part in.''

Her words finally brought a smile to Nathan's face. He leaned back in the chair imagining Faith with that icy schoolteacher-stern look she wore so well. The one that made him want to move in close, press up against her to see if he could lick away the frost, make her melt beneath his mouth.

''Mildly amusing activities?'' he protested. ''Lady, you've got to be kidding. I've never strained and grunted and worked so hard just to pick up a damn pencil, just to manage to grasp the phone before the person on the other end decides to give up. And yes, I know what you're saying, but I—hell, it doesn't change things. I'll wait until you have time for me, Faith. If I have to backtrack to make up for lost time, that's no problem.'' *Not if it meant he could steal a few extra days of time with her trying to recover the ground he'd lose.*

The thought sneaked in. He ignored it, suppressed the knowledge that he was being a jerk again, that he was being unreasonable and foolish. He tamped down the niggling thought that maybe another therapist would be the best course, that if Penny Damen was competent, then he should switch to her completely. But no, Anderson had done his homework. He'd insisted Faith was the one. Nathan blew out a breath of relief.

''I'll wait, and you're not to feel guilty. It's my choice.''

''Nathan...''

''You don't have any recourse. Just . . . watch your boy. Make sure he gets well. Call me when he's better.''

"Nathan . . . please, I wouldn't do this if there was any other way. No way would I turn you over to someone else's care if I could be there. I don't like this, either."

Her voice sounded tired, sad, concerned. Nathan thought he could hear a small cry in the background. Faith covered the phone, murmured something soothing, reassuring.

Hell, what kind of a louse was he? Didn't she have enough problems, enough worries without him giving her grief? Hadn't he already proven that he knew how to make a woman miserable?

Nathan let the pain rip through his gut, welcomed it. He took a deep breath. "All right," he said wearily. "You win, but don't send anyone else. Just stay put. If you won't let me wait, I'll come to you this time. And we'll take as long as necessary. You can tend to your son whenever you need to."

"Mommy . . ." He heard it then, closed his eyes against everything that word meant, all the feelings it evoked.

Nathan could sense Faith's concern, the fact that she wanted to go to her son, but she wasn't too happy with the way this conversation was going.

"I'll call you back," she promised.

"No, don't bother. I'll be there. And don't worry about how. I'm a doctor, remember? Used to dealing with sticky situations. Besides, my hands are starting to work a bit, doing what I tell them. Someone's been teaching me things."

"No, Nathan, I'll call you."

"I won't be here. And don't worry. Tend to your boy. He needs you now." And with that, Nathan hung up, dropping the phone into the cradle.

He looked at the phone, knowing she'd call back and that he couldn't ignore her if she did. It was time to leave.

The door seemed ominously large and threatening. He hadn't gone anywhere in forever. He hadn't really *done* anything in forever. And he definitely couldn't remember doing anything *for* anyone in a long, long time.

Maybe he shouldn't be doing anything now. Going to Faith was damn stupid, risky. Hell it was insane, it was too much involvement, something he'd regret tomorrow, something he'd have to face eventually. But not today, at least not yet.

Faith looked down at her son, listlessly pushing his truck around and around the table leg. The seat of his superhero pajamas drooped and she automatically reached to snug the stretchy material up around his waist. He was small, her son, her little superhero. And when he was sick, he seemed even smaller. The urge to shield him from life was stronger than ever at such times. All her protective instincts bubbled up.

But today she was feeling even more protective, more tense than usual. Nathan had said he was coming to her house. Nathan, who had once ordered her not to bring her child around, whose eyes filled with desolation at the very thought of facing a four-year-old had volunteered to come here, knowing that Cory was home.

And Cory, who'd decided his "daddy" shouldn't be a doctor because of Nathan, because Nathan kept his mother away from him at night was going to have to share his space with the doctor he so resented.

Yes, Faith was definitely feeling tense, protective. She wanted to keep Nathan and Cory apart. It would have been better if the two never had any chance of meeting. This was bound to be upsetting for both of them.

"Cory?"

The little boy looked up from his truck and turned dark, listless eyes to her own.

"Cory, in a little while, Dr. Murphy will be coming over. You know who that is?"

His solemn nod was answer enough. Faith lowered herself to the floor, cross-legged, and pulled her son onto her lap. She wrapped her arms around him and began to rock. Dropping a light kiss on the top of his head, she felt the slight heat in him. It was almost time for another dose of acetaminophen.

Cory sighed and snuggled his back in closer. "Big boys do not get rocked," he announced, even as he settled his head into the cleft where her forearm met her body.

Faith kissed him again. "You know that's not true. When they're sick even big boys get rocked. It's part of the treatment. It's part of what helps you get better and makes the sick part not quite so bad."

"Is that what you do with your patients? The ones that are sick? Like that doctor guy that's coming over?"

Faith smiled against Cory's hair. He was so transparent in his jealousy, so much the wistful little man.

"No, silly," she whispered into his scalp. "You know that you're the only one who gets this super extra special kind of treatment. But... I did want to talk to you about Dr. Murphy before he gets here."

"What about?"

"Well..." Faith draped her arms more closely about his own. "You know how you're scared of things sometimes?"

Cory tilted his head back, considering the question. "Like monsters... the ones that hide under the bed?"

"Cory... you know there aren't any monsters..."

"I know, Mom, but still..."

"Okay, all right, like monsters, then. Well, sometimes grown-ups have things that scare them, too."

The deep brown eyes that stared up at her narrowed suddenly with suspicion.

"Are you afraid of monsters, too?"

She touched her nose to his. "Didn't I just tell you that there are no monsters?"

Relief tinged his small smile. "Okay, maybe snakes then."

Faith tilted one shoulder. "*Maybe* snakes. But that's not what I'm talking about. Sometimes people, for their own reasons, are afraid of things that don't seem scary at all to most of us. Like Dr. Murphy, for example."

"He's afraid of something? But he's a man."

"Being a man doesn't make any difference at all, Cory. Even the strongest man is afraid sometimes. It's all right to be scared at times. It's normal. But Dr. Murphy, well, Dr. Murphy is, maybe not afraid, but he's...uncomfortable around children. You know what I mean?"

"He doesn't like kids?" Cory's voice was filled with disbelief, and Faith felt a faint sense of release, of satisfaction. Cory's own father hadn't wanted him, hadn't liked children at all, and yet her son was so secure. He knew nothing of rejection...yet. She hoped to high heaven that he'd still be so blessed by the time this evening was over.

"Um...well, it's not so much that he doesn't *like* kids, but they make him nervous. Okay?"

"I guess so."

"So, what I'm saying, Cory—" she shifted him in her arms so he was facing her completely "—is that I'm going to give you your medicine, and when the doorbell rings, I want you to crawl into bed—or if you're not sleepy—I want you to play quietly in your room while the doctor's here. All right?"

"So I won't scare him?"

She nodded. "Sort of. Yes. And I'll come to you just as soon as he's gone. Can you do that, do you think?"

He studied the situation a second or two, then slowly nodded, climbing off of her lap. "I 'spose so."

Cory trailed Faith as she went to the locked cabinet and took out his medicine. He made a face when the cherry-flavored liquid went down, then allowed himself to be led off to bed.

"Mom?" he asked, his little brow furrowing. "If that doctor's scared of a little kid like me, what do you think would happen if a real monster came through the door? I mean, I always thought that men, that daddies, weren't scared of stuff, but I don't think this one would be much good in a 'mergency, do you? Maybe you better put that down on the list when you get a chance. Put down 'not scared of kids or monsters,' okay?"

"Bed, Cory," she ordered, trying to stifle her smile. "And yes, I'll put whatever you want on the list. For now, you just skedaddle off to bed."

He nodded, climbing under the covers. "Okay, but if I wake up, can I play with the little piano Mandy brought me?"

Faith frowned. He really should be getting some rest, but she felt guilty for forcing him into confinement during Nathan's visit. And it wouldn't be for long, anyway. "If you play quietly," she finally agreed. "And if you start feeling sick, if something's really wrong, you call me, all right?"

"Like if I have to hurl?"

"Hurl? Cory, where on earth did you get that term?"

A cough convulsed his small body, making the blankets shake. Faith moved forward, putting her arm about him, soothing his skinny little frame with long strokes of her hand.

Looking up at her with red-rimmed eyes after the coughing spell had passed, Cory tried a smile. "I saw it on TV, Mom. Don't you ever watch TV?"

She did, now and then, but Faith couldn't help thinking once again that Cory was watching entirely too much, and possibly watching things that were inappropriate for a four-year-old. If she had her way, if she was with him all the time... but she wasn't. She'd just have to speak to Mandy, that was all, Faith thought as she tucked Cory in and left the room.

But talking to Mandy would have to wait. For the next few days, Cory was home sick. And for the next hour or so, Faith's mind was going to have to be concentrated on someone other than her son. On Nathan.

She sat down to wait and wondered why she suddenly felt so nervous. Last night was over, past. It was nothing, just like she'd told him. That kiss had meant nothing, nothing at all.

Faith's house was small, very small. As if the architect wanted to build a model before he moved on to the real thing, Nathan thought as he pulled his car into the long, narrow drive. Made of plain white clapboards, the house sat well back from the street, a well-tended yard stretching out to the side.

Nathan wondered if the yard was what had sold her on the place—he remembered she'd said how much she liked green—or was this simply all that she could afford? That last thought nagged at him, reminding him of how she'd told him that she had no choice but to accept him as a patient.

It wasn't a pleasant thought, the fact that Faith had been forced to take him on, but he didn't have time to dwell on this. The door flew open before he'd made it up the steps. And the look on Faith's face wasn't one of welcome.

"You drove?" she demanded, motioning toward the big Suburban parked out front. "Who gave you permission to drive?"

Nathan was still standing on the second step down from Faith. And from here, he could look directly into her eyes, see them darken with frustration.

"You're saying I needed to ask your permission before I rented a car and got behind the wheel, short stuff?" he asked, wanting to see if he could make her bristle even more.

He did. She was. At his implication that she was taking her role too far, Faith's chest began a rapid rise and fall that lifted the soft yellow cotton of her blouse, brought her breasts close to his chest. Or maybe it was his use of the outrageous nickname that had set her off. Or his nearness, the sudden realization that the last time they'd been this close, he'd been on the verge of losing all control, of sliding his palms up under her blouse, seeking skin, resting his hands beneath the heavy fullness of her breasts, then—

Nathan frowned at his fantasies. Faith wasn't even looking at him, her attention was pointedly on the car. It wasn't his closeness that was disturbing her breathing. The woman was angry, just plain angry. And all because he'd gotten behind the wheel of a car without calling her first.

The thought made him smile. "Lighten up, Faith, it wasn't that big a deal once I got my hands on the wheel," he said, stroking one finger across her mouth to ease her frown away.

Immediately she stepped back. "You could have been hurt," she insisted, moving aside to let him in. "And now I'll bet you think you're going to drive home when it'll be dark by the time we're done. Well, you can just chase that thought down the wind, Dr. Murphy. You'll leave here in a cab.''

"Dr. Murphy?" he asked. Wow, the woman really was miffed.

"Forget it, Faith," he reiterated. "I made it behind the wheel once. I'll be fine from now on. Like I said, it was nothing. And Dan was with me when I leased the thing, anyway."

His last comment effectively shut her up. Rolling her eyes, she turned to lead him to the table she had set up for his session.

"You know, I really am beginning to wonder about Dr. Anderson," she said. "He makes it far too easy for you to get around him."

"That's why I have you, Faith," Nathan told her. "To make sure that I don't get away with a thing."

*Bad choice of words, Murphy,* Nathan told himself, watching the faint hint of pink creeping up Faith's neck. His words brought back too many memories of the night before, when he had definitely been trying to get away with something. But he could see she wasn't going to mention it, wasn't going to say a word. He had to give the woman credit for control. She should've let him have it with both barrels.

She had swirled all that long hair up onto her head today. The way he'd once wished she would, thinking she'd be less enticing with her hair out of sight. But he'd been wrong. With her hair piled high, the long length of her neck was exposed, visible, all gleaming, vulnerable skin. Pale ivory that peeked through under a wisp of a curl that had slipped down.

Faith must have seen the way his eyes trailed up the slope of her shoulder to her naked jawline, her earlobe, for her blush deepened just a shade. She cleared her throat. "So, you did okay, then? Driving, I mean?"

"Fine," he agreed, submitting his hands for her inspection. No way was he going to tell her that when he and Dan had taken possession of the Suburban, a cold sweat had broken out over his body, that he'd practically had to force himself into the driver's seat. And that once he'd climbed inside, he'd sat there for long minutes, gasping for breath, his head resting on the steering wheel.

Dan had suggested that they might take it slowly, simply practice sitting in a car for a few weeks, get a therapist involved.

That was all it took, the thought of letting someone else into his life. He was barely surviving Faith, would scarcely make it through to the end of his time with her. He'd closed his eyes, snapped the belt closed, started the engine. Things hadn't been "just fine" but he had driven, nonetheless. He was here, in one piece, and he'd driven himself. Somehow, he would manage to get home again. He wondered if Faith realized how hard he'd had to fight not to glance to the empty passenger side of the car, remembering the accident and all that he'd lost.

She must have. There was still that look in her eyes, the one he was sure a thousand patients had seen. Worry, caring, concern. Those emotions flowed from Faith as naturally as raindrops sliding down a slippery windowpane.

"Well, that's good then," she said simply. "It means you're one step closer."

"Closer?"

"To recovery. To getting back your career, your life."

But he would never get back his life. Not ever. It wasn't even something he dreamed about. It wasn't even something he wanted.

"Come on," he said, holding up his palms. "I know you're dying to start torturing me after I've argued with you so much today. Let's go. Make me squirm, Faith."

Her face was sun-kissed pink, her eyes a dangerous dark aqua when she reached out to him. He'd meant to antagonize her, to get her eyes to flash. Anything was better than that butter-warm look of concern she wore so well, the look that really did torture him. Because it made him wonder what a life with a woman like her would be like. And that was the kind of thinking he wouldn't allow himself.

"You want torture, Murphy?" she asked, sliding her hands onto his. "You want to start doing things without consulting your therapist first? All right then, you're going to have to show me some real progress. We're going to sweat and strain today. You're going to show me just what you really can do with these hands, Doctor. I want to see a hint of the man who made magic in the operating arena."

But she was smiling as she said it, no rancor in her voice. Because she really did intend for him to operate again, Nathan knew. Because she really did have faith in his abilities. It was a humbling thought, a terrible thought.

And damn it, he wasn't going to let her down.

Nathan worked.

He worked until he thought that his hands would start shaking and, abruptly, Faith pulled back. As if she'd known.

"Time for a short rest, then you show me what you're doing at home before we call it a night. I'll be back in a minute."

She was going to check on her son. He knew that, had figured the boy was sleeping when he hadn't heard a sound from the rest of the house.

Now, with Faith gone, Nathan circled the room, not sure what to do, not really wanting to stare at her stuff, to see what the real Faith Reynolds was like. He knew the therapist, but this was the woman. And the therapist was dangerous enough.

But still, he looked. Lots of flowers in the house. Lots of white wicker. No toys in this room. No trace of her son at all, except for the pictures hanging on the wall. Dark hair, dark—very dark eyes, with a smile that said "Look at me, Mom! I'm the happiest kid alive."

Quickly Nathan turned away... and came face-to-face with Faith. A wary, worried Faith. And he didn't want her to worry about him.

"Nice-looking kid," he said with a phony smile. "Doesn't look like you, though. Not at all."

"No." She relaxed a bit at his smile and his easy conversation. Nathan knew suddenly that she'd put all her son's toys away for his sake, because of what he'd told her that first day, because of Amy.

"No," she repeated. "Cory looks nothing like me. He's Jim through and through... physically, anyway."

Her words sent Nathan back to the picture, looking at her boy, trying to see the man who'd fathered him, who'd been married to Faith.

"Your ex-husband, does he still live around here—or maybe you're widowed?"

He turned to see Faith leaning against a wall, her arms crossed tightly across her chest. "No, I'm not a grieving widow, Nathan. And Jim doesn't live around here, either. Truthfully, I don't know where he lives."

Probably not an uncommon situation, yet her words startled Nathan. Looking at Faith, knowing what he did of her, seeing the photo of her son, he couldn't imagine a man, even an ex-husband, not staying in the picture, somehow.

"He doesn't see your son?"

She blew out a long puff of air, twisted her lips up into a cynical smile, straightened to a stand. "No, he doesn't see him, and he hasn't. Not since the day Jim walked out, just after Cory was born."

Nathan started to speak, felt his brows bunching, the rage building toward a man who could simply walk away from this woman, leave her to raise a child alone. But Faith held up one hand, silencing his criticism.

"Don't be angry, Nathan. I'm not anymore. Or at least not too much, too often. Jim was—well, he wasn't a bad man, he was just very weak, didn't know what he wanted. I didn't know what he wanted, either. I didn't understand that he didn't really want a wife, a child, that he needed me for the moment, not for eternity. But it was long ago. I've had time to adjust. And he did, after all, leave me the best part of himself. He left me Cory.

"Now, come on. I've talked too much about me, and it's really you we're here for today. Let's finish up."

Her husband hadn't known what he'd wanted, had left her, hadn't been there for her when Cory was growing up? A molten surge of anger flicked through Nathan's body. How could a man be so blind, so unfeeling? But then...had he been any better? The times he'd been gone, working, when his wife and child had needed him at home? The times his love had lain on a shelf while he tended to his work. Who was he to judge? And yet if Jim Reynolds had been standing here right now, Nathan knew he'd have to fight to keep from clamping his less than perfect fingers around the man's neck.

Hell, it was a good thing the man wasn't here then, Nathan thought, shaking his head. Somehow he didn't think that Faith would consider strangling her ex-husband a legitimate form of therapy. No matter how much it challenged the weakened muscles of his hands.

It was probably better to stop thinking and just get back to work as Faith had asked.

But even as Nathan flexed his fingers, clenched his fists, felt the strength that hadn't been there mere weeks ago, a small thud came from the other room.

Faith looked up, excused herself and pushed up from the table, rushing away.

Nathan could hear the murmuring from the next room, the hushed, childlike sounds. He could hear the low, caressing tones of Faith's voice.

Faith came out, closed the door. She moved back to the table and took Nathan's hands again.

The silence lasted maybe two minutes.

And then Nathan heard it, the faint, muffled, off-key tinkling of a tinny toy piano. The high, fragile voice of a little boy singing. Made up verses, not loud. Or at least not loud by kid standards. Nathan remembered that there was a difference in what an adult considered noisy and what a child did.

"I am tired of being sick, but soon I'll be better, yes, soon I'll be better. My mommy said that I'd be better really, really soon," the little boy voice wailed, squeaky and off-key.

Nathan looked up at Faith, saw that her eyes were wide with apology, her hands held tightly, her body frozen as she looked at him.

The song was abruptly interrupted by a short burst of husky coughing. Then, "And when I'm better I can go outside, go outside, go outside. And I can go to the park." The tinny tinkle of the piano keys went on, nowhere close to the melody the boy was trying to carry. "Not today, but real, real soon."

It was a silly song, a pathetically small song, soft and somewhat lispy and totally without musical merit. But Nathan could see that child as if the door were made of glass, as if he himself had developed X-ray vision. He'd bet money that Cory was swaying, playing, lost to any sense of the rest of the world as he sang on, taking the words as they came to him.

It was a song that made Nathan's heart hurt, brought tears to the back of his eyes. He'd had a child once who sang like that, who sang every day of her life. One he'd give his own life to hear again. But he wouldn't hear her. Not again. Ever.

Looking up, Nathan saw that Faith had come out of the statuelike shock Cory's first words had cast on her. Moving quickly, she hurried toward the bedroom door.

Nathan knew what she was doing. She was going to stop the music. She was going to ask her son to be quiet. To protect him, her patient, a grown man. A man who'd silenced another child's songs once before.

"Faith. Stop." He held out his hand to her, even though her back was turned to him. His voice had been loud, louder than he'd intended.

Slowly she turned around, a question in her eyes. "I'm sorry, Nathan. Don't worry, I'll be back. I'm just going to—"

"I know what you're going to do. But don't. Come back. Now. Leave him alone. He isn't hurting anything. He isn't hurting *me.*"

It was a lie, a whopper of a lie. Lord above, he was hurting with every single childish note. But it didn't matter. He would hurt a great deal more before he'd silence that child. He wasn't going to stop the little boy's songs. He wasn't going to ever hurt a child again—not if he could help it.

It was clear that his words had made a difference. Faith's too-tense face relaxed and she smiled. It was clear that she'd been worried about her child, that this situation hadn't been easy for her, either. And now that she knew the little boy's presence wasn't going to send him into some kind of a rage, she seemed more like herself. The weight was gone. And only Cory's intermittent coughing tightened the muscles of her jaw. Twice she left to check on him.

"I'll be back tomorrow, Faith," Nathan said, as he was rising to leave a few minutes later. He didn't know where the words were coming from, or why. This was *not* the kind of day he wanted to repeat. "You shouldn't have to be away from your son when he's sick, and it's clear that this thing's going to last a few days. It's the flu, after all."

She looked up at him as though he'd just dropped a bucket of gold dust in her lap. As if he'd just given her a gift. He wondered just how hard it was to raise a child alone. Damn hard, too hard. The words bounced back at him.

But the exultant look on her face vanished in a heartbeat.

"Yes, it is the flu," she admitted. "I should have never let you in the door. What if *you* get sick? How am I going to feel then? Heavens, I don't know what I was thinking of today, my head must be on crooked. You should *not* be here. There are germs, lots of germs. I'm probably already infected and you've been sitting across from me for the last hour. Maybe if you stay away tomorrow—"

There she was, the ultimate therapist, worrying about him, putting his needs before hers again. Nathan knew that if he left her to her own devices, she'd be calling him in the middle of the night, sending Penny Damen or some other therapist, trying to protect him.

"Germs?" he asked, with a sudden grin. She'd used the word as a weapon, trying to chase him away.

"Germs. Lots of them," she repeated, crossing her arms, wearing that fierce expression he'd come to look forward to.

"And you wouldn't want me to take any chances, huh?"

"No. Definitely not." She shook her head vigorously.

"Well, then." Nathan stepped closer, pinning her crossed arms against his chest as he took her lips with his own. It was a swift kiss, hard and crushing, then turning soft and gentle before he moved away. This woman drove him crazy, made him nuts, made him do things he knew he shouldn't, that he'd absolutely promised he wouldn't.

"Germs," he agreed. "Now I've got them, too. So don't bother trying to palm me off on some other therapist, Faith. It's you and me to the bitter end, or it's no one."

He left her standing there, staring wide-eyed, shocked, her fingers pressed against her lips as though she couldn't believe he'd touched her again. Hell, he didn't believe it himself.

But he had. He could still taste her on his lips, still feel the warmth of her body snugged up tight against his. The woman-soft fit of her...

It had been stupid to touch her again, foolish to say that he was coming back tomorrow when tonight had been tough enough. If he had an ounce of brains, he'd call her back, tell her he *did* want another therapist in spite of what he'd said.

He should. He knew he should.

Especially when, on the dark, night road, the memory of a small, wispy voice came to him. Faith's eyes watching him. The little boy singing. It was wrong to think of that. Dangerous. Scary. *Wrong.*

And as he drove on, nearing his home, the place he'd hidden away in for so long, the voice followed him. He heard Cory's voice over and over, small and soft and insistent.

If he went back to Faith's home, Nathan knew he'd have to learn to live with that voice, with that little boy in the next room. It was the way of things. Kids couldn't keep still and silent. They needed to squirm and gallop, they needed to try out their lungs. Nathan knew. He'd had his Amy.

The thought of going back and facing that child again alarmed him, sent razorlike chills chasing up and down his spine. But there was something else, too. Relief, a small speck of relief that even though Amy was gone, there was a child somewhere, who brightened the heart of a woman. Somewhere, there was still a child who sang.

Tomorrow he'd have to face that child, face Faith and her son head-on. He could no longer pretend that the boy didn't exist.

Nathan pulled into his drive, cut the engine, climbed out of the car and slapped his palm against the hood. Reality washed over him.

Memories. Faith murmuring to her son with love. Faith standing there shocked when he'd kissed her. Faith. Cory. Together.

And he'd be right there in the midst of it. Watching. Feeling, damn it, feeling.

He'd definitely send her flowers when it was all over. He *would* celebrate, glad when everything was done and he could stop feeling again.

Faith, but when you go to Boston, I'd see about this spe...

He leaned deep into the chair, crossing... one of his ...
"Fine," he said, keeping... guard mode. ... back ...
into her arms for the first time since... this morning, she ...
willed away the tension. Most of the time, Nate spent...
nothing, just sat on... a word. Faith... without...

... but soon she'd... ... the ...
"No," she said simply. "I... realized that even ...
an explanation.

... he wasn't ... to succeed...
... believed she ... now. ... I'm ...
... ... the next...
... the wrong ... of his mind...  and I'm okay with

## *Chapter Five*

The man had guts. She had to give him that. Faith watched Nathan try not to flinch as Cory called her for the third time in thirty minutes.

Still, he didn't say a word, just sat there tensing his fingers. Somehow Faith knew that this was less a form of exercise than a very real gut reaction to her son's plaintive cries.

"I'm sorry," she apologized, sitting down again after seeing to Cory's needs. "I thought he'd be feeling better today. But with this cough—well, he's just not used to his body rebelling on him this way."

"Don't sweat it, Faith," he told her, as though she were the one who was sitting there talking through gritted teeth, as though she were the one with an allergy to small children.

"I should never have let you talk me out of getting you an alternate therapist," she said. "This can't be helping you much, not when you're so obviously tense about this situation."

His laugh, deep and laced with cynicism, caught her by surprise. "Lady," he said, leaning forward, staring straight into her eyes. "I've been tense since the moment you walked into my house. And so have you. You open your mouth and I back you up against a wall. I argue with you and you lean into my face. And when we touch—"

"Don't," she said suddenly, "I've explained that to you. It's gratitude."

"Gratitude," he agreed. "And I don't want to discuss it any more than you do. I just want you to know that I'm taking it. All of it. This makes no difference. That little boy in the next room—" Nathan lowered his voice. "This is his territory, his home. I'm the intruder, and I'm dealing with the situation."

But at the next tiny little moan from Cory, Faith couldn't help looking into Nathan's eyes. She saw the too-deep breath he took, the way he swallowed convulsively.

"Mom?" Cory called.

She bit her lip, cast Nathan an apologetic glance.

He slid his hand on top of hers. "Go to him, Faith. He's your son. You don't owe anyone, least of all me, an apology for wanting to protect him. He's a little boy who's sick. He needs his mother with him and his things about him— including his teddy bear."

Faith nodded at the last words. She'd thought she'd managed to snatch the small, grubby bear up from the couch and hide it behind her back before Nathan had noticed. The little bear had *kid* smudged all over its worn-out fur. How foolish she'd been to think that Nathan wouldn't have honed in on something like that with the speed of a heat-seeking missile.

"All right, then, I'll try to stop feeling like a guilty parent," she promised.

Nathan turned her hand over, palm up. He traced her lifeline with the pad of his thumb. "Then there's no problem," he said softly. "Go on, now. I'll bet the fever is making him thirsty. And take your time. I'll still be here."

Slowly Faith withdrew her hand from his. She moved away, then turned back slowly. He was watching her. His eyes locked with her own.

Swallowing, she took one small step backward. "You must have been one hell of a wonderful father, Nathan Murphy," she whispered.

And whatever light had been in his deep green eyes died. The shutters were down. Nathan's jaw tightened. "I was the world's worst father," he said, his voice cold and clipped. "Worst husband, too. I was hardly around for Joanna and Amy at all. Furthermore, when that car broadsided us, I was at the wheel. If I'd been paying attention, if my mind had been on my wife and child's safety the way it should have been, I might have avoided the accident. I could have gotten us out of the way, or at least whipped the wheel and turned the car, taking the brunt of the impact myself. I could have saved my wife and little girl. So no, don't think that Faith. Don't think anything good about me. Just get out of here and go to your son. Now."

Nathan watched as Faith slipped from the room. He listened to her murmuring soothingly, calming the fretful little boy. His gaze followed her when she moved to the kitchen. He heard the slam of the refrigerator door, the rustle and clang of dishes. And beneath the cover of noise, he heard the small, anxious voice. "Mo-om?"

Another clatter followed, pans falling. The phone rang. A muffled "Oh no!" and then a long, low sigh from Faith. It was clear she couldn't hear her son's call. It was also abundantly clear to Nathan that the stress of worrying about Cory, and about himself as well, was taking its toll on Faith. There were circles beneath her eyes, her face was drawn, her lips tight. He'd bet the bank that she'd barely gotten any sleep last night.

"Mom, you there?" The voice echoed again, followed by the creaking of the bedsprings.

Nathan looked toward the kitchen. He knew he should call her; she'd want him to do that. But one glance around the kitchen doorway, at her slender, bowed back was enough. One glimpse of the exposed curve of her neck bent in resignation as she held tight to the phone, picking up the things she'd dropped, and he knew he wasn't going to call to her. She needed a break.

And he could give that to her—maybe. If he could just force himself into that bedroom, if he could just steel himself to see what the boy wanted. It wouldn't take much. Really, it was such a simple thing to do, wasn't it? So, why was he shaking? Why was his heart tripping along like a clock gone haywire?

Nathan took one step toward the door, then another. Slowly, so slowly. The room seemed far, too far away and yet too close at the same time.

Another step. Just a few more and he'd be there.

The bed creaked again. If he didn't stop him, the child would be running around, bare feet and all, forced to go search for help when help was standing here shaking on the wrong side of the door.

Taking a breath, pulling his shoulders back, clamping down his jaw, Nathan forced himself past the threshold, forced himself to look toward the bed.

His eyes locked with a pair of small, dark ones. Suspicious eyes.

The boy coughed once, then bit down on his lip, snuffled his pajama sleeve across his nose. "Are you the doctor? The 'portant one?"

Nathan twisted one side of his mouth up in a quick grimace. "I don't know about that important stuff, but I'm a doctor, all right. Looks like you're one pretty sick guy."

Cory studied Nathan suspiciously. "I got the flu," he agreed. "I wanted my mom, cause my sheets is all crooked and I can't find my bear. But you should go now. The flu is 'tagious, and my mom says you're afraid of boys like me, anyway."

The child frowned and turned away, hunching his skinny little shoulders as if Nathan would disappear if he wished hard enough. It was clear that he wanted nothing to do with the "'portant doctor." And that if Nathan was smart, he would take this golden opportunity to back away. It was also clear that he was one miserable little tyke. His cheeks were too rosy, his eyes big, bright hollows of darkness. His fever was readable without even using a thermometer.

Nathan crossed his arms, slid his hands into his armpits. He studied the boy's words. "Your mom said I was afraid of you, did she?" He could hear Faith's steps as she moved from the kitchen tile onto the muffling carpet.

"Nathan? Cory?" Faith's voice was worried. In just a minute she'd be here. Nathan took one more look at the anxious child caught up in the tangled sheets, then his gaze passed over the room. It was brightly decorated, cheery, yet small, very small—and boxy. He felt he was sucking up all the space just by standing in the doorway, and Nathan wondered if Faith had only been guarding his own feelings by insisting the child stay in here. No, she loved this kid too much, but still...a room this size made a man want to bust down walls with his fists. He wondered if the boy felt the same.

He stared down at the small, tousled head of hair, noticed the tiny pink toes that had come untucked from the dinosaur sheets. The bed seemed narrow, too tiny a space to have to stay in for long. When Faith moved into the living room, the child would be alone, sick, lonely....

Nathan shifted with his thoughts. He shouldn't have come in here. Faith had been right to keep the two of them separate. Looking down into the boy's dark, anxious eyes, seeing the miniature hand that fisted around a bunched-up bit of sheet, Nathan knew he didn't want to be around this kid. It would be torture. Even now his heart was thudding painfully, trying to push back the memories of other little fists that had clutched his neck tightly. With hugs and squeals of laughter, and soft little-girl, raspberry jelly kisses.

The boy sucked in his lower lip, an utterly childish gesture that brushed at Nathan's memories. A small cough started up, shaking the fragile little body, holding him in its frenzied grasp.

Faith rushed in at that moment, moving to the bed, smoothing her hand in slow circles over the child's back and then hugging him close when the angry coughing finally ceased. "You okay, Cory? Better, love?"

Small hands slipped around her waist, the child's face hidden against her body.

Faith looked up at Nathan, tilting her head. "Nathan? Are you—I—I wondered where you'd gone to. I—"

He shook his head. "No apologies, remember? You couldn't hear him when he called. I figured I was capable of helping out a little, anyway."

Her cheeks pinked slightly at his words. He knew that she was feeling guilty, irresponsible again. But she simply nodded. "Thank you."

When her gaze locked with his, and he looked into those huge blue green eyes Nathan felt the room shrink even more. His chest felt tight as though some of the air had been sapped from the meager supply available in this tiny space. What air remained seemed highly charged.

He felt the change when the boy turned to look from him back to his mother. Pulling on Faith's sleeve, Cory stared forlornly down at his messed up sheets. "I losted my bear," he said sadly.

Faith smoothed her hand across her son's hair. She slipped to her knees beside the bed and helped him straighten his covers, hunting out the bear that had slipped off the far side. Kissing him on the forehead, she snuggled him close for one brief second, then looked back at Nathan. "I'm sorry I'm so disorganized today. Let me just get Cory set up here and then we'll get back to your session."

She pushed one tense hand through her hair, sending a wayward curl flopping down onto her forehead. Nathan noticed the spot of spilled juice on her pale peach blouse, the fact that her mouth was tight, her whole body was stiff as if it would dissolve, melt away, if she let up on herself for one second. He noticed the way the boy's eyes grew worried when his mother mentioned leaving him alone.

With an internal shudder of resignation, as he mentally closed his eyes to what he was proposing, Nathan reached out and picked up the glass of juice she had put on the nightstand. He held the drink out to Cory, looking down at the little boy who was studying him so rebelliously.

"I'm not afraid of the flu even if it is contagious," Nathan said, giving the child the small plastic tumbler. "Why don't we take you into the other room so that you can be near your mom?"

The sudden hopeful look in the kid's eyes nearly sent Nathan spinning away. It was such a small thing he had offered. Such a small, stupid thing.

"Mom says I have to stay in my bed," Cory said, chewing on his lip. "Little boys who are sick must get lots and lots of sleep," he reminded the man, obviously quoting his mother.

"Then you'll just have to *get* lots of sleep, won't you? I expect those eyes to drift shut just as soon as we get you set up on the couch. Doctor's orders. Grab your bear now while I carry you. Can't have you getting chilled."

And without waiting for Faith's reaction, Nathan reached down and bundled the child, blankets and all, into his arms. He barely weighed more than a puff of air, so there was no reason for a man Nathan's size to feel his knees buckling, no reason for him to feel that the other room was two million miles away, as if he'd never make it. Taking a deep breath, Nathan turned and strode toward the door. He could feel Faith close behind him, but he didn't stop, not until he reached the blue-and-white checked couch. Gently, forcing himself to go slowly, he lowered the boy to the sofa, then stepped aside to let Faith tuck in her son.

Faith moved to her child, plumped up his pillows, smoothed the sheets and blankets, then whispered a kiss across his brow. Soft, gentle, loving. But when she rose to her feet, when her glance moved to Nathan, the softness died and turned to exasperation.

"Could we talk for just a second before we get back to work? In the kitchen, perhaps?"

She had moved close, dangerously close, and Nathan breathed in the soft lemony scent of her, indulged himself for a few brief seconds, even though he recognized the fight in her eyes.

Shrugging, he followed her lead, ducked into the bright red-and-white kitchen.

As soon as they were out of earshot she turned to him, clasping her elbows as if she'd blow apart if she didn't hold on to herself.

"I thought we talked about control when we first began these sessions, Nathan. I was worried that you might be a bit high-handed, but you haven't been, at least not much. At least not until now. That was some move, Murphy. I'd like to remind you that Cory is my son, my responsibility, and right now he's sick. He needs to be in bed, he needs his rest...."

"He needs his mother at his elbow," Nathan corrected, moving closer, close enough to feel the tension radiating from her, close enough to touch...if he thought he could handle it. "Besides, Faith," he continued. "If you think he's gotten one iota of rest since I've been here, then you and I must be using a different definition of the word. On the other hand, I'd be willing to wager that he'll rest a whole lot easier now that he can see you, and realize that I'm no threat to him."

Faith skated back, moving out of touching range. She turned away and fiddled with a loose knob on a cabinet. "He knows you're no threat to him. I told him so."

"All right, but maybe he needs to see that for himself. Besides, maybe you misinterpreted my actions. Maybe I have my own selfish reasons for wanting the boy in there with us. If you don't have to keep jumping up and down like a jack-in-the-box between the two of us, we'll get more done. I'll be able to complete my sessions faster. And you know how much I want to get through this. After all, I promised you roses, didn't I? To celebrate the end? Are you saying you don't like roses?"

She turned large, suspicious eyes on him. "I adore roses, Nathan. I can't wait for you to be better so that we can celebrate with flowers. But how about your convictions? You told me at the beginning—no children. Sharing a room with Cory will be very difficult, won't it?"

Five seconds of silence. Then Nathan shrugged. "I'm a surgeon, Faith. And dealing with kids is a part of that life. I'd damn well better get used to it."

No point in telling her that he was restricting whatever future practice he might have to adults. No point in letting her know just how really difficult this was going to be.

"All right, then. I'll thank you, Nathan, no matter what your reasons were. These last few days have been hard for Cory. For me, too. I hate not being able to help him. So, thanks. Now, come on, let's get back to your hands." She took a step toward the door.

"All right, but...not yet. I have a question." He touched one long finger to a tawny curl of her hair, stopping her progress as effectively as a granite wall.

Turning slightly, she looked back over her shoulder. She stood there waiting, suspicion shining in the depths of her eyes. "Ask then," she said softly.

"Your boy...Cory, he'll be home for another few days?"

Her nod was long and silent.

"In the daytime, when you're here—that is, the hospital, they're not giving you any grief?"

Faith swallowed, looked up at him, her teeth worrying her lip. "No one's said anything, but I do have to go back. Cory's sick, but not as sick as he was. And I can't take more time off. Tomorrow...tomorrow I'll take Cory to the children's center at the hospital. I can't take him back to the sitter while he's sick."

"The children's center? He's been there before?"

She nodded. "Once, a year ago. Just for a day." Faith's voice had dropped, becoming whispery and strained. It was obvious that she wouldn't be taking her son to some impersonal children's center if she had any other choice.

But when Nathan moved closer, held out one hand and then dropped it again, opened his mouth to speak but found he had no words of comfort to offer, Faith held out her own hand to stop him from saying anything. She took a deep breath, pulled her narrow shoulders back in a gesture of determination, and faced him head-on.

"Don't talk about it anymore, Nathan. I don't want to. Besides, the clock is ticking and you're wasting time. Did you plan on giving me those roses in this lifetime or didn't you? Don't you want me out of your hair, Murphy?"

Lord, yes, he did. He wanted her out of his hair, out of his life, his thoughts, his dreams. He wanted a world where he had never met her, a world where the scent of lemon didn't remind him of a woman's lips moving beneath his own.

"You'll get your roses, Faith. Just as soon as I can manage it."

When Faith moved back into the living room, Cory gave her one long, solemn stare. Then he smiled slightly and turned on his side. Within five minutes he was breathing the short, shallow breaths of a fevered, sleeping child.

From her seat at the table, she looked up at Nathan who was still standing. His gaze drifted around the room, taking in everything but her sleeping son.

He'd said he wasn't a good father, that his child's death was his fault. And yet, he'd been careful with her son, gently bundling him up to keep him warm, carrying him into the living room when there was nothing at all wrong with Cory's legs.

Why? Was he paying his dues, doing penance for the past? Faith didn't know, and it was as clear as calm water that Nathan wasn't about to explain his actions—wasn't at ease with those actions. He'd stepped away quickly when he'd finally deposited Cory on the couch. He'd been kind, but uncomfortable. She'd been more right than she'd thought when she'd told Cory that Nathan was afraid of children.

"You're too quiet, Faith. Are you . . . are you worried about him?"

Nathan hadn't looked Cory's way, but it was obvious who "him" was.

Faith couldn't hide her small, exasperated smile. The man wasn't going to let it alone. "Do doughnuts have holes, Nathan? Of course I'm worried about him. I worry about him all the time. *All* the time. But Cory and I have been through this before. We'll go through it again. And again and again. So don't worry. As you said, we'll deal with his illness, and this isn't really anything you need to concern yourself with, so don't go looking at me like that."

"Like what?" His green eyes stared into her own, so intently that Faith wanted to slide back in order to escape their dangerous pull.

"Like—like you're thinking about bundling *me* up in blankets and ordering me off to bed, too. I'm not four years old, Nathan. The words *doctor's orders* don't intimidate me."

A small chuckle escaped Nathan. "If there's one thing I know about you, Faith, it's that the word *doctor* doesn't phase you in the least. But I do know some words that are upsetting to you. Words like *children's center*. You don't want to leave him there, do you?"

Nathan's words pricked at her conscience. Slowly, she blew out a breath of air, bracing her elbows on the table.

She pushed her fingers through her hair in a gesture of frustration. "It's not a bad place," she said softly, miserably. "Not at all. They have toys and games there. The staff is friendly, committed."

But the words she hadn't said were the ones that haunted her. The children's center was a nice place, but it was in a hospital, part of a large, sterile institution, and Cory had been scared the last time. He'd only been three...and he'd cried for her—miserable sobs she'd continued to hear long after she'd gone. And Cory almost never cried.

"I've stopped in there," Nathan stated. "They make every effort to make the kids comfortable. It's a workable solution when you have a sick child."

Faith nodded. "That's what I've been telling myself. And it won't be for long, anyway. Less than a week. By next Monday, Cory will be fine, and able to go back to pre-school. He can stay with Mandy again in the afternoons. He feels safe with her."

Nathan reached out and touched Faith's jawbone with one tense finger. "You're a good mother, Faith, so don't look so guilty. There's nothing more that can be done."

*There's nothing more that can be done.* Nathan was still saying those words when he turned to leave—when he was finally forced to walk past the couch and look at the child.

The blankets had bunched down around Cory's waist. He was sleeping on his stomach, his small behind sticking up like a baby's. His teddy bear had gotten crammed down between the cushions, and Nathan knew the boy would be looking for it again when he woke up.

Without hesitation, Nathan pulled the small bear free, lightly laying it by the child's hand. When the fluffy fur touched the boy's fingers, he shifted, pulling his legs higher beneath him, blinking his eyes open sleepily.

"You going?" he asked groggily.

Nathan nodded. "I'm going. You go back to sleep. Get your rest so you can take care of your mom, okay?"

"Okay, Doctor," Cory agreed, snuggling back into his covers, closing his eyes again. "See you tomorrow."

"See you tomorrow...Cory," Nathan finally answered. *See you tomorrow.* But not before the boy had made his trek to the hospital, not before Cory had spent the day in a strange place filled with smiling strangers and antiseptic smells.

As Nathan edged around the door and started down the walk, he turned to look once more at the house and saw her. Faith was framed in the doorway, all eyes and tawny hair and softness. She was an incredibly strong woman, one who wouldn't let life beat up on her, who wouldn't let a small setback stop her. So why did she look like a frail, beautiful flower torn from the stem? Why did she look as if she needed someone to hold her? And why, damn it to hell, why in the world did he find himself wanting to run back and wrap her in his arms, promising he'd protect her with his life, that he'd be her guardian, when he knew damn well that he wasn't made of the right stuff for that role?

Faith closed the door, and the light went off. But still Nathan stood there, watching the house for long minutes before he got into his car and drove off.

There was a full moon shining. It should have been a bright and sparkling night, a good night for a drive. Clean and fresh and promising.

Instead, Nathan could only picture the little boy, snuggled in his dinosaur sheets, resting peacefully in his safe, warm cocoon. He could only hear Faith's worried voice. *It won't be for long. It won't be for long.* He'd wanted to do something to reassure her that her son wouldn't be sad or scared because of the decision she'd been forced to make. But in the end he'd said nothing, had let her go back and face her doubts alone.

She *was* alone. She had no one else to watch her sick boy. No husband. No one to turn to.

Nathan wondered if that was the way it had been for Joanna, having a mostly absentee husband, a man too caught up in work to stop and offer to help.

Braking at a light, he thumped the wheel with his palm. He couldn't do anything about Joanna, he couldn't change the past.

And he couldn't help Faith, either. He couldn't. It was impossible, unthinkable.

What she needed right now was an alternative, a baby-sitter she could trust. He couldn't help with that. Besides, there was no way she would trust *him*, not a man who'd argued with her, fought her, kissed her when her guard was down.

He wasn't the one for this job.

But as he drove on, Nathan couldn't help remembering another child, another anxious mother. He and Joanna had taken Amy to the emergency room for stitches. Amy had clung to him, whispering frantically. "I'm scared, Daddy. I'm scared" she'd said as tears rolled down her pale cheeks.

It wasn't the same, not at all. Cory was going to a bright, well-stocked child care center, not an emergency room. It wasn't nearly the same thing.

Except that Cory was a child. A small, sick child. And therefore, more easily frightened than usual.

Then there was Faith. A woman who'd had far too much stress in her life lately, a fair share of it coming from him. Faith, who was so worried and tried not to let it show.

Swearing beneath his breath, Nathan pulled into his drive. Turning the car around, he drove back the way he'd come.

Her house was dark when he got there. Nathan moved around to where he knew Faith's window would be. He rapped lightly, and called out in a low voice, afraid he'd wake the boy or scare Faith.

Her light flicked on. She peeked out the window and pulled up the sash. Nathan could see that she was wearing a soft white robe that covered her from neck to knees. It was the kind of thing that was supposed to look demure, but only made a man want to pull it off to see what was hidden underneath.

"Nathan?" she whispered, shoving her long, loose hair from her eyes. "What's wrong? Come in." She bent out the window, motioning him toward the door. "I'll let you in."

"No." He placed his fingers over her soft lips to stop any words that might follow. She gazed up at him over his fingers, her blue eyes still hazy from sleep.

"Faith, I had to come back. I've been thinking. Cory— he shouldn't have to go to the children's center. That's not right. Not when I've got nothing to do all day. So, if it's okay with you, I'll come stay with him tomorrow. Hannah will be here part of the time, too. I've called her and she has a few hours she can spare. You can leave the boy at home then. He could stay in bed, with his own things."

She was wide awake now, her eyes following the movement of his lips. Leaning out into the night, she reached up and touched the stiff line of his jaw, the one he'd been holding rigid ever since he'd made the decision.

A small smile lifted her lips. Slowly she shook her head. "I couldn't let you do that."

"Because you don't trust me? I thought that might be it. That's why I thought of Hannah. She's got lots of kids of her own, grandkids too."

Faith mimicked Nathan's actions, sliding her own fingers across his lips. "It's not because I don't trust you,

Nathan. I *saw* how gentle you were with Cory. It's because of you. Being with Cory—you don't want that. Not really."

"I won't lie to you, Faith." Nathan spoke, his lips brushing against the pads of her fingers just before she moved them away. "The very thought scares me, it's hard to look at any child and not see my own, not remember my own failings. I'm a man with regrets, Faith, lots of regrets. And I know how much you're worried about your boy, wondering if he'd be scared staying in the hospital. If I could have saved him that and didn't, well I think I'd have a whole lot more regrets tomorrow than I do today. I can't afford that, Faith. I don't think I can afford even one more regret in my life. Besides, I could probably keep him happy for just a few days. Hannah will be around when she can, and Cory will rest a lot. I'd treat him right, I promise you."

"I know that," she whispered. "I trust you."

He shook his head, but she stilled him as her hands framed his face. "Will this take away the guilt about Amy?" she asked.

Nathan slid his hands up to clasp Faith's wrists. "Nothing's ever going to erase the past. I'm never going to forgive myself. But if I can help you—well, you've helped me. It's only right. It's something I need to do."

Her smile transformed the night. She leaned close, and quickly dropped a feathery kiss on his lips, her mouth warm and giving against his own. "Then, thank you, Nathan," she whispered. "I accept. I probably shouldn't, but I will."

Nathan stared at her. He streaked one finger across his lips where her own had rested just seconds ago, then touched her mouth. "Gratitude?" he asked with a smile.

"Gratitude. It works both ways," she agreed.

"I'll see you in the morning, Faith. Early," Nathan said, stepping away. But he waited for her to lower her window and throw the catch to lock things tight before he drove away.

When he climbed into the car his mind was reeling, remembering the feel of Faith's lips against him. She'd kissed him, touched him voluntarily, for the first time since she'd seared him with her palm that first session weeks ago.

But it was only because she was grateful, he told himself.

He could still taste her on his lips—her innocence, the warm, wild scent of her. And he wondered how in the world he could continue on. How was he going to make it through the next day or two with her son? How would he make it through the next weeks with Faith?

Because if anything was clear to him, it was that he deserved nothing from Faith Reynolds. Not her gratitude. Not her trust. He didn't deserve it, and Lord above, he didn't want it. Because when a man had a woman's trust, he could abuse it, lose it. He could lose her....

Maybe he could take care of her child for the next day or two and still stay sane. But there were limits to what a man could survive.

Having experienced Faith's kiss, Nathan figured that he'd just about reached his limit.

It was time he started putting in double duty on his therapy. It was time to start ending things between him and Faith. But first he had to get through tomorrow.

# Chapter Six

With a full day ahead of her, Faith knew she shouldn't be up, wandering the dark house in the middle of the night. Yet she was.

Ever since Nathan had come rapping on her window—no, ever since she'd looked into his eyes and seen his warmth and his concern written there, ever since she'd laid her lips against his—her heart had been beating out of control. There was no way she could go back to sleep now.

She'd already had a cup of warm milk and honey, watched a whole hour of guaranteed-to-make-anyone-snooze reruns on TV, and still her bed offered no relief.

"Faith...what were you thinking?" she whispered, groaning.

She'd kissed him, knowing that it was the last thing in the world she should be doing. Hadn't she learned her lesson, watching her mother get her heart trampled? Hadn't she herself married expecting what could never be? But at least she'd had an excuse then. Jim had claimed to love her, he'd vowed to stay with her.

That wasn't the case with Nathan. He made no secret of the scars on his soul, the ones that wouldn't let him give too much of himself, that wouldn't let him take, either. He had regrets, he'd said. He would always have regrets. They crippled him emotionally. A woman would be ten kinds of a fool to let herself feel anything for such a man...and Faith had already been a fool. She wasn't going to be one again. She knew that there were paths down which a woman shouldn't wander.

She'd told Nathan that Jim had only needed her for the moment, not for eternity. Just as Nathan needed her for only the here and now. She had to remember that, really remember that. She couldn't afford any more kisses in the night.

Accepting his offer to watch Cory was probably crazy, too...but that was where all her intelligent plans fell apart. She couldn't refuse his offer and take Cory to a strange place when there were good people willing to care for him in his own home. She couldn't have risked her son's tears—not even to protect her own heart.

Rising from the couch, Faith moved to her son's room. His bear had fallen again, and she placed it beside him in case he needed it in the night. As he stirred in his sleep, she gently eased away.

"Don't worry, angel, there are no monsters, just Mom," she whispered. The sound of her voice was like a drug. The frown eased from Cory's forehead and he slept.

Picking up the empty glass from his bedside, Faith noticed a scrap of paper on the table. It was Cory's list. She'd promised to add some details to it.

Taking the paper out of the dark room into the light, she looked at the items written down so far. *Black hair and brown eyes. Not a doctor.* Smiling to herself, she grabbed a pencil and added Cory's latest request. *Not afraid of kids or monsters.*

This was the man in her future and Cory's, the man who was going to be a father to her son. *This was the man she'd spend her nights with some day.* The thought sent a shiver through Faith. A vision of Nathan rose up before her, and she remembered the trembling that had shook her when he'd held her, touched her. He was so tall, so strong in spite of his injuries that when he'd wrapped her in his arms she'd felt surrounded, overwhelmed by the need to burrow deeper within his embrace.

But the man on this list wasn't Nathan, she thought, tapping her pencil against the paper. She didn't want it to be, and neither did Cory—her son had made that clear already. Surely he'd forgive her if she added a few words of her own...because tonight she needed something. She needed to feel safe.

Picking up the pencil again, Faith bunched her brow, deep in thought. Finally, the lead wavering over the frayed bit of paper, she scribbled one word down.

*Short.* It seemed ludicrous, laughable even...but it was something. It solidified her vision of the man. Short with dark hair and dark eyes. A man who wasn't afraid of anything, a man who wasn't a doctor, who couldn't ever be Nathan Murphy in a million years.

An immediate sense of peace washed over Faith. She slid the paper onto the end table, switched off the light, and laid down on the couch.

But when the first bright shaft of morning sunlight hit her, Faith moaned, raking her fingers through her tangled hair.

She'd spent the night reaching for sleep, trying to envision a short man with dark hair and dark eyes; one who

would come to her, love her child, who would stay with her
and Cory for always. She wanted to find that man, wanted
to latch on to him in her dreams.

But in the morning, neither dreams nor sleep had come,
and the only man she'd been able to think of had green
eyes . . . and he was tall.


Nathan watched as Hannah packed up her bag. The
moment that he'd been dreading had come. Hannah had
made lunch, but now she had errands to do. She was leaving, and soon he'd be alone with the boy.

Hannah had helped him past the awkward first moments this morning. She'd been here for Faith's instruc-
tions, she'd fed the boy his breakfast, helped him when he'd
needed it. Now, however, she was leaving.

"Well, I'm off, Dr. Murphy. You call if you need me, but
things should be all right. He's fed, he's slept most of the
morning. All you'll have to do is keep him happy till his
mother comes back in a few hours."

And that's what Nathan was dreading the most. Keeping Cory happy meant talking to him, listening to him, *being* with him . . . for hours. This time he couldn't avoid the
child. He'd offered to help Faith, promising her that she
could trust him with her son. And that was what he had to
do. But his breath was coming fast and hard, his hands were
trembling as though he'd spent all morning working them
when in fact he'd done nothing.

Nathan waved Hannah out the door, then moved to the
living room where Cory was stretched out on the couch
again.

The boy looked up when he entered. Warily, it seemed to
Nathan.

"Do you—do you need anything?" Nathan asked, hating the harsh sound of his voice.

Cory bit his lip and shook his head.

"You're sure?"

The child's nod was slow, but very, very distinct. He didn't want anything...except for this man to leave him alone. Nathan could tell.

Well, the kid was well set up. Surrounded by books, toys, that ugly little bear, he looked as if he could hold out for a while, but the room—it was so damn dark in here.

Nathan moved to the curtains and started to draw them back when Cory called out.

"Don't open them." The boy's words ended on a squeak.

"You could use some light," Nathan said. "It's not good to stay in the dark all the time." *Like I had until Faith came along,* he reminded himself. "It's a sunny day, sun's good for what ails you," Nathan assured the child.

"Is zat more doctor's orders?" Cory asked, an anxious tone to his voice.

"Definitely," Nathan agreed. "Why don't you want the curtains open?"

For five full seconds he thought that the kid wasn't going to answer him. Then, with his chin pushed out defiantly, the little boy opened his mouth. "Sometimes, maybe...a monster could sneak in—you know, if he knows we're here. But if the curtains are closed—"

Nathan saw the slight tremble in the child's lip, heard the quaver in his voice. He knew that denying the boy's words would be wrong. "I see," he said, letting his hand drop from the cream-colored drape.

With only a slight pause, he moved closer to sit on the end of the couch. "Have the monsters been bothering you this morning?" he asked.

"No." Cory nervously fiddled with the wheel on a yellow dump truck. "Cause Hannah stayed in here with me, but you—I told you, Mom said—"

"I know." Smiling slightly, Nathan stopped the boy's words. "I remember. Your mother told you that I'm afraid of boys."

"Are you? Are you afraid of kids? Mom's 'most always right." Cory nodded emphatically and leaned forward.

Nathan found he couldn't keep his own gaze steady. He turned his attention to the pattern of the carpeting instead. Cory's overflowing love for his mother was too great a reminder of just how innocent and trusting a child could be. *Too* trusting, sometimes, he remembered. Some parents weren't right, or good . . . or even there when they were needed most. Nathan knew that too well. Still, he wasn't the one Cory was talking about.

"Your mom *is* usually right, isn't she?" Nathan agreed, knowing Faith's penchant for honesty. "But maybe what she meant was something a little different. The truth is that—well, I haven't been around children for a long, long time. I wasn't sure I'd be comfortable talking to a little boy."

"You're talking to me." Cory stopped twisting the wheel of the truck and stared up at Nathan, wide-eyed and waiting.

"You're right, I am. Guess that means I don't have to be afraid of you, doesn't it? Just like you don't have to be afraid of the monsters. I'm here with you, and you don't have to worry. I'll keep you safe, Cory."

It was a promise to himself as much as it was to the child, and the sudden adoration that bloomed in the little boy's face at those words nearly made Nathan gasp and move away. He forced himself to stay seated.

"So, you're *not* afraid of monsters, then, are you?" the child declared, sitting up straighter.

Nathan thought of all the things he was afraid of—children, a woman like Faith. She could make him want things he'd never allow himself again, like love and home and family. Yes he definitely had his own monsters. He knew the meaning of fear.

"No, I'm not afraid of monsters," he lied, knowing how badly the boy needed the security of his words. "But I once knew a little girl who was very frightened of them."

"What did she do? Did a monster get her? Is that why you don't know her any more?" Cory's eyes were two round disks. He sucked in his lower lip, waiting.

*Did a monster get her? Yes, oh yes.* "No, a monster didn't get her," Nathan promised. "Because her daddy got rid of all the monsters in her house."

"He did? Did he fight them with a sword? Did he shoot them with a gun or zap them with a phaser?" Cory was leaning forward now, the truck forgotten. His fingers clutched the sheets.

Nathan shook his head, slowly. "No, nothing that violent. Her daddy went to the store and bought some antimonster paint. He painted the inside of the little girl's room, and the smell of that paint was so bad that the monsters couldn't stay, not even in the other rooms in the house. The smell of that paint just drove them away completely. Monsters hate it, you know. They hate that antimonster paint, because once it's on the walls, monsters can't live there for, oh, at least another fifty years. It's pretty good stuff. If you're into getting rid of monsters, that is." Nathan leaned back, watching the child's face.

A small light entered the little boy's eyes. He swallowed once, hard, then started to speak. But as he opened his mouth, a strangled cough came out. He brought his hand up to his lips to catch the next one and the next, great choking coughs that racked his small frame.

Rising quickly, Nathan went into the kitchen, catching his fingers into the loop of a cabinet handle, then grasping a plastic cup and filling it with water. He could hear Cory's frantic coughs in the background.

Rushing back to the boy, Nathan wrapped an arm about the child's shaking shoulders, lifted him and held the cup to his lips. Water spilled onto the sheets, but a small amount made it into Cory's mouth.

Cory drank a little, coughed some more, his tiny body stiff with the strain. Nathan could feel the heaving of the child's muscles beneath his own hand, which was trembling now that the warmth of the child's body had seeped through to his fingers—now that he realized what he was doing.

It was enough to set off a string of memories, back to a time when Amy had been sick, and he and her mother had taken turns rocking her in the night. It had been one of the few times he had been there to tend his daughter when she'd been ill. One of the last times, Nathan realized.

The memories were so vivid, so real. He wanted to run from the room, to take his hand from the boy's back, and leave.

But at the next lingering cough, the child's body jerked with the effort as he tried to speak. And Nathan did the only thing he could do, the only thing anyone who'd ever loved a child could do. He relaxed his hand, and began making slow, soothing strokes over the boy's back, stopping only long enough to give Cory a small sip of water now and then. Nathan uttered low, meaningless words, words meant to comfort. To reassure the child . . . and himself.

"It's okay, Cory. You're going to be fine. Everything's going to be fine."

As the hacking slowly ebbed away, Cory turned dark, watery eyes to Nathan. Sweat beaded his brow and Nathan pushed the child's damp hair off of his forehead.

"Dr. Murphy?" Cory whispered.

"Yes, son. What is it?"

"Do you think Mom has any of that paint? The anti-monster stuff?"

Nathan smiled, a small smile, but a smile nevertheless. He had made it through. And while he still didn't feel easy being with the child, he was at least getting by.

"I don't know if she has any, Cory. Not that many people know about it. But I promise you one thing, we'll get some. And we'll slap it on your walls. You won't have a thing to worry about anymore. We'll get rid of your monsters."

If he could only get rid of his own so easily, Nathan thought. But no, there wasn't a paint in the world that could change the past. His own monsters, the ones that lived inside him, were here for always. He didn't deserve to be free of them.

When Faith opened the door of her house the first thing she noticed was the strong smell of latex paint. The next thing she noticed was Nathan's long, lean frame sprawled out on the floor, next to the coffee table shoved up against Cory's couch. Nathan appeared to be winning big time in a game of Cootie.

She watched as he worked to position the plastic insect's leg and poke it into the correct hole on the body, the last piece towards completing the puzzle and winning the game. Interesting. She'd bought the game for Cory on a whim and he'd lost a number of the pieces, so that she'd wondered if it had been such a hot idea. Now, watching Nathan try to manipulate the small, slippery bit of plastic, she gave herself a mental pat on the back. And she gave Cory credit, too. Maybe taking care of her son *wasn't* such a bad idea. Maybe she should take Cory along on her therapy sessions, if he'd come up with this unique way of getting Nathan to practice manipulative exercises.

"You win, Nathan, you win," Cory announced as Nathan finally managed to push the pieces together.

Nathan looked up at that moment, straight into Faith's eyes. He held up the small plastic insect which promptly wobbled and fell apart.

"Well, I *did* manage to get it together," he said, half laughing, half defiantly as he looked down at the pieces now lying on the floor.

"*And* you won," she pointed out with a grin.

"Yup, he did, fair and square," Cory agreed, wiggling around on the couch.

Nathan's face turned a deep shade of pink. "Fair and square? Not likely, squirt. You know you let me win so that I could have at least one triumph." Smiling at Faith, Nathan held out his hands helplessly. "Your son felt sorry for me. He beat me at this blasted game ten times running."

"Nathan is not very good at Cootie," Cory pronounced solemnly, turning to his mother.

"That doesn't matter, Cory," she said, sitting down next to her son. "Everybody has some things they're good at and some things that are more difficult for them. You're very good at this game and at making up songs. And Nathan is a doctor. He's good at helping people get better when they're sick or hurt. In fact he's very good at it, one of the best."

"*And* he knows how to get rid of monsters," Cory added. "He painted my room with antimonster paint. Now we don't have no monsters."

"Any monsters," Faith corrected. "So, that's what that smell is."

Nathan was rising to his feet, looking slightly sheepish. "I hope you don't mind that I painted Cory's room. I had

Hannah stop and pick up the paint. It's just white, the same as before."

"I don't mind at all. Not if you've gotten rid of the monsters," she said, watching Nathan's eyes. "Have you?"

He stared down at her, letting her read what was written there. "We've gotten rid of Cory's monsters, yes," he declared.

But not his own, she could tell. It was as plain as white paint. He had survived the day with her son, he had banished her child's fears, and that had to be enough.

She would accept that, because she had to. With a small nod, Faith stood and moved a step closer. She took the remaining plastic game piece he held in his hand and gave it to Cory.

"Then, thank you, Nathan," she said quietly, trying to ignore the warm feeling that had thrummed through her when her fingers had brushed Nathan's palm. "Thank you very much."

She folded her fingers closed to mask the heat and turned away quickly, concentrating on her son and the scattered remnants of the game. "It's time to clean up the table, Cory. I think you're well enough by now to move around a bit more, and I'm going to make dinner. There must still be some steaks in the freezer."

"I'll say my goodbyes then," Nathan said, moving to the door. "And be back here in about an hour and a half. Is that enough time?"

Faith didn't answer. She waited until Cory had waved a cheerful goodbye and trudged off to put his toys away before she turned to Nathan. "You think I'm such an ungrateful slouch that I'd send you out to find your own dinner after you watched my son all day?"

Nathan raised one hand, easily now. Faith noted that he no longer felt the need to hide his hands behind his back or shove them in his armpits. "I didn't expect payment for watching Cory. I volunteered to stay because I needed to."

"Because you didn't want any more regrets in your life."

"Yes," he said, the sharp line of his jaw tensing.

"Good." Faith crossed her arms in a stern gesture, rising on her toes to bring her eyes closer to his level, but she couldn't keep a partial smile from forming. "Then everything's fine, and you'll stay for dinner. Because leaving when I'm trying to thank you will definitely land you in hot water, Murphy. You'll have regrets, big time. I'll—I'll—" She tilted her head, trying to think of something dastardly enough to convince him to stay.

Nathan took a step closer. "You'll what, Faith? What will you do?" he whispered.

"I don't know," she admitted with a tiny, weak shrug, angry at herself for wanting him even nearer. "Give everyone at the hospital your address and tell them you want visitors? Get Cory to call you up and sing songs all night? Set up a tent outside your door and stage pajama parties for a week? Maybe ask Dr. Anderson what he's holding over your head?"

At his sudden frown, she shook her head. "No, I'm sorry I said that. I didn't mean it. You know I wouldn't do that, but . . . darn it, Nathan, the man who rid my house of monsters forever is not walking out of here without dinner, and I *do* mean that. It's absolutely final, Murphy. Therapist's orders. So, are you convinced yet? Are you scared yet?"

Nathan stepped even closer. He studied her as he braced his hands on the counter next to her hips, bracketing his legs around hers. "Am I scared? Of you? Of a woman I tower over, a woman who threatens me with pajama parties?" He placed his lips near her ear. "Absolutely, Faith. Absolutely. No woman has ever stripped away my defenses the way you have. No woman has ever scared me more."

Nathan's last words were spoken with conviction, his voice husky, whisper soft and caressing. His breath feathered across Faith's cheeks. She believed him, but knew that she was just as frightened of what was happening between them as he was. And now she'd teased him too much, pulled him too close with her taunts again. It would be best to let him go home for dinner. It would be best . . . but then he'd be alone. . . having his dinner in an empty house, as he had for so long. . . .

"Just tell me if you're staying, Nathan," she finally said, trying to keep her voice from wobbling, trying to manage to look mean when they were so close she wasn't sure where her body ended and his began. "Are you staying?" she repeated, "or do I have to haul out the heavy artillery?"

She swallowed hard. Her emotions were far too near the surface, in danger of being exposed. The need to lean close and press her breasts against his chest was frightening. The desire to splay her hands across the broad planes of his back nearly overwhelmed her.

"We're just talking dinner, Nathan," she whispered. "You know that I don't want more than that. No more than you do. I'm your therapist, here to do what's good for you, and eating a big dinner is definitely good for a man who's been faced with kid food all day."

Faith managed a small smile. Nathan was still close, his hips nearly brushing her own. Nervously, she sucked in her lower lip, trying to ignore her own body's inclinations.

Nathan groaned softly. "Stop doing that. Stop looking like it's you I'm having for dinner, Faith. I'll stay, I promise, if you'll just stop staring at me like that. Only don't bother with the steak. I hardly think a little antimonster paint merits such a first class spread."

Slowly, he straightened. He backed off to give her space and room to breathe—room to think.

"That's nonsense, Nathan," she said, moving to the fridge to pull the steaks from the freezer then popped them into the microwave to defrost. "You have no idea how long these steaks have been up here. They ought to be tougher than old retreads by now. You'll get some real practice wielding a knife, which of course, you need. You are a surgeon, after all."

She looked back over her shoulder to see if Nathan was playing along, if the tense mood of moments ago had been broken. He was standing just a few feet behind her, one side of his mouth tilted up slightly.

"And you're a devious and dangerous woman, Faith. Trying to manipulate a man."

At his words, Faith sobered and she turned to him quietly. "No, not really, Nathan. I'm just trying to thank you. You helped Cory today. You helped me. Cory seems so much brighter, more relaxed, and you did that. Can't you accept a simple thank-you from me without fighting it every step of the way?"

Nathan opened his mouth—to argue, she was sure—but she reached out and brushed her fingers across his warm, dry lips to stop him. "I'm only offering to feed you, Nathan. Don't you deserve at least that much?"

Her fingers were still resting against his lips. Gently Nathan pulled them away, held her hands against his chest. She could feel the soft give of skin, the hardness of muscle, the rise and fall of his breathing. He held her that way for long seconds, then turned her hands palm up, and released them.

"I'll stay and practice my cutting skills on your steaks, Faith," he said.

It was a victory of sorts, although Faith couldn't help noticing Nathan hadn't really answered any of her questions. He didn't think he deserved thanks, she knew that. And because of that, she couldn't help asking just one more question.

Busying herself at the stove, she waited until she heard Cory singing in the distance, knowing that they wouldn't be interrupted. She didn't turn around because she didn't want to make Nathan feel cornered.

"Nathan?" she called softly, knowing by the tingles up her spine that he was still close behind her.

"What, Faith? Do you need some help? Just tell me what you want."

She paused, knowing that she was delving into things that were really none of her business. But she wanted to know, needed to know, why Nathan had given in to her bullying that first day at his house. He was a man who'd been hiding for a long time. Faith realized she'd been pushy, but she was wise enough to know that obstinance alone just wouldn't have cut it. Nathan had been forced to the wall. Somehow.

"Nathan, what exactly *is* it that Dan Anderson is holding over your head? I said I'd never ask him, and I won't, but... are you in trouble in some way? Does it have anything to do with your medical practice? Do you need—do you need help? Is there anything I can do?"

There was no reason he should answer that question; absolutely none. She was nothing to him, really, and he was a proud man. There wasn't any way he would really let her help him beyond what she was already doing. She knew that, yet still she had to offer. Whatever it was that Dr. Anderson knew, it was important to Nathan. And a therapist had to keep a patient's total sense of well-being in mind, all the time, she told herself. That was why she was interested, why she wanted to know. That was all.

"Nathan?" she asked, softly, finally turning to look at him. "*Is* there anything I can do? I'm here to help you, you know. You don't have to say anything if you don't want to, but you *can* trust me. I won't betray your secrets."

Nathan's eyes darkened. "You think I don't know that? That's the problem with you, Faith. You give too much, you offer too much. You're a devoted therapist, Faith, but it isn't wise to leave yourself so open. People can hurt you... *I* could hurt you."

She swallowed, keeping her gaze anchored on his. "Does that mean that you don't want to confide in me?"

"Yes—no. It's not that. Hell, I suppose you *should* know. Then you can find out just what a jerk I really am. What Dan threatened me with, it's nothing... and everything. It's about my sister, Celine. I've been lying to her ever since the accident. She thinks I'm fine, completely healed. She believes that I've been back at work all this time."

Faith held out one hand, not quite understanding what he was saying. "Why?" It was the only word she could manage.

"Why didn't I tell her? Why don't I want her to know? Because she'd come. In a second. Celine is—" He held out his hands and shrugged his shoulders. "Celine is family. She *has* a big family. Five wonderful children, who think she spun the stars. She's the epitome of the very word *home*—warm, nurturing, a real mother hen. If she knew the truth, she'd fly here on the first plane she could catch. And if she came she'd bring—"

"The kids?" Faith supplied.

"And more." Nathan took a deep breath. "Pictures, tears, sympathy, hugs, chicken soup, smiles... memories.

She'd dredge up the memories, *all* the memories," he ended on a husky growl.

"And you can't take that, can you?" Faith asked softly. She wanted to go to him, to put her arms around his waist and offer him all the things he'd just told her he didn't want from his sister. Somehow Faith managed to keep her distance. "You can't take that at all, can you, Nathan?" she repeated. "The family, the memories?"

Silence slipped into the room, the only sound the small and distant chatter of Cory playing with his toys.

Finally Nathan shrugged. He ran one hand over his jaw, ignoring her question. "I'll take what you're offering tonight, Faith. Therapy... and steaks," he promised.

But no more than that, Faith realized. Never any more than that, tonight or any other night. Whether he had meant to or not, Nathan had sent her a warning. One she meant to heed.

Nathan had gone and Cory had been sent to find his pajamas when he appeared at the door to Faith's room.

"Mom?"

She looked up to see Cory. He was still dressed, a familiar bit of paper clutched in his fist. He was looking at her with that complete love and trust that only small children know.

This was what she needed, Faith thought with a sigh; a moment with Cory, a moment to look ahead to a future that didn't include Nathan.

"Mom, you need to change some stuff here," he explained. "I got a problem."

"A problem, tiger? What could be wrong?" Reaching out, she took the paper from him, and drew him closer to her chair.

"Read the list," he said, looking confused.

Faith cleared her throat. *"Black hair and brown eyes. Not a doctor. Not afraid of kids or monsters. Short,"* she concluded.

"Short?" Cory squeaked. "I didn't put that."

"No." Faith was surprised to find herself blushing. "I did. Well, after all, I'm kind of short myself," she reasoned, defending herself. "It would be hard to spend my life looking up at a giant."

Still Cory frowned. "It's no good," he concluded, shaking his head. "I need to change some stuff."

"All right," Faith said carefully, taking up the eraser end of the pencil he offered, leery of what was coming next. "Shoot, tiger. Tell me what you want to change."

*"Not* short," he said immediately. "Don't worry, you'll grow, Mom," he promised. "And cross off 'Black hair and brown eyes.' Maybe it would be more fun to have a daddy who *didn't* look so much like me. You can leave 'Not afraid of kids or monsters,' though. That's still okay. And then—"

"Cory." Faith knew what was happening. She knew what he was going to say next. "Let's not make so many changes all at once. We have time, lots of time. I told you. And you put a lot of work into this list. Let's leave it till another time, when it isn't so late, and we're feeling fresher."

She could tell by the stubborn set of his chin that he was going to argue. Gently she tapped him there with one finger. "Please, Cory. Mom's tired."

It was a cheap comment, almost a lie. But she couldn't have faced the final disintegration of this list, the words she'd clung to only last night.

"Okay," he finally agreed. "But read it to me one more time, and point to each one as you read it, so I'll know for sure what it says."

With a nod Faith touched the paper and read the list. "Not a doctor," she said, pointing to the first line on the list. "Not afraid of kids or monsters," she concluded. "Now are you happy?" she asked.

Cory looked skeptical. "Just one more thing," he begged. "Just one."

Giving in, Faith let out a sigh. "Just one," she agreed, and poised her pencil over the paper.

"Put down, 'Doesn't have to be good at Cootie,'" he said solemnly. "Because I can teach him," he explained. "I am very good at Cootie."

He *was,* this child of hers, this bright-eyed boy. And he was very good at something else—heading for heartbreak.

"Cory," she said softly, not wanting to kill his newborn hope, but knowing she had to. "Dr. Murphy cannot be your daddy. He just can't."

She half expected Cory to argue, but to her surprise he didn't. "I know, Mom," he said. "When Hannah got the paint, she said it was a real shame Nathan wouldn't marry up again, cause he'd make a good husband. He can't be a daddy for me if we don't get married, can he?"

"Hannah said that, did she?"

"Uh-huh. To Nathan. He frowned at her real big, too. But I heard. I didn't ask no questions, so Nathan wouldn't frown at me."

"I see," she said, unwilling to explain more to him. "So why are you changing your list?" she asked, holding it out to him.

Cory shrugged and took the paper from her hand. "Maybe, Mom—maybe there's somebody else like that who knows about monster paint. Like on TV when the guy has a twin he never knew about. Maybe there's somebody else just like Nathan."

Her son really *had* been watching too much television. But at the moment that seemed the least important part of this conversation. Faith caught herself latching on to her son's wishes. Maybe there *was* someone out there just like Nathan.

But no. There was no one like Nathan. And soon there would be no Nathan at all . . . in Cory's life or in hers. That was the whole point of therapy—to treat the patient and let them go. And that was what she needed to remember from here on out.

# *Chapter Seven*

Two days later, as Nathan was about to leave Faith's house, she informed him that Cory was now germ free, and ready to get back to his normal routines.

"Thank you so much, Nathan," she said, holding out her hand, "for watching Cory these last few days. I'll call Mandy tonight and make arrangements to drop Cory there on Monday morning. Since she'll be taking over the evenings, too, I'll be by your house at the usual time."

Nathan looked at her hand, slender and small, outstretched in an impersonal handshake. That hand had made him ache with physical pain at one time, when they'd first started working. Faith's palm had rested against his own, offering encouragement and instruction. But she'd also touched him, several times, with gentleness. And he'd known the pleasure of those hands against his chest while he plundered her lips.

Now she was all business, all primness and formality. Just the way he'd always wished she would be. He didn't want to remember the way she twisted him up inside whenever they touched, knew he ought to just accept her polite gesture and clear out. Still . . .

Nathan ignored her hand and looked down into her eyes. He felt a sheepish smile lift his lips. "Are you telling me I'm fired, Faith?" he asked.

Slowly Faith lowered her hand. "Of course not," she said, a confused expression on her face. "But we both know that you were just doing me a favor, filling in for a few days when I was up against the wall with no one to watch Cory, and—"

Nathan reached down and picked up Faith's hand at last. He patted it gently, trying to prepare her. "*We* both knew this was just for a few days," he admitted. "But apparently Cory was a tad mixed-up about the conditions of my employment. It seems—" Nathan stopped, cleared his throat, feeling the slight burn of embarrassment "—it seems I've somehow committed myself to a few more days with him."

"A few more days?" she asked, pulling her hand back and folding her arms. She narrowed her eyes in that suspicious way that Nathan knew so well. "How many more days?"

"A few," he repeated. "I'm not sure. It depends on the wind. I promised we'd go kite flying and . . . oh, a few other things. Not many," he said, holding up one hand defensively.

"Nathan, Nathan . . ." Faith drawled softly. "Why on earth did you promise him that? I know you don't want to spend any more time with us than necessary. I know this hasn't been easy for you."

"Yeah, well, I survived," he admitted. "And this situation really isn't Cory's fault. He was sick and grumpy and I wouldn't let him watch any more television. When he got tired of playing Cootie, I bet him three cookies that he couldn't win another game. Things—well, things got a little out of hand after that.''

Faith was rocking on her heels now, enjoying his discomfort as she tried to hide her smile behind her hand. "You're telling me that you gambled with my son in a game you know you really stink at? Nathan, shame on you.''

Nathan frowned and ran a hand along the line of his jaw. "I don't know how that kid does it. It's a game of chance, for Pete's sake. How can I keep losing every time?''

"I don't know," Faith said soothingly. "Honest I don't, but don't worry. You're not going to abide by a promise that was made on a bet. And you're not playing any more Cootie with my son. I love him and it's a cute game, but heavens, I never thought those little bugs could be so dangerous. Don't worry, I'll tell him all bets are off.''

"Not on your life, lady," Nathan said, stopping her from going to Cory by placing one hand on her shoulder. Gently, he grasped her forearms, turning her until she faced him completely before he let her go. "I may not have always been the kind of man I should have been, Faith, but I stand by my word. Cory won fair and square. I'll stick to my end of the bargain. Besides, he's—he's such a bright little guy. I hate to see him...well, nothing against his baby-sitter, Faith, but that woman seems to know far too much about a remote control and not nearly enough about what kids should be doing with their spare time. It won't hurt me to take him on a few outings, get him into the fresh air.''

"You're right." Faith groaned, sliding her arms around herself as if to ward off the truth. "I knew Nathan, I *knew* he was watching too much television, missing out on the good stuff, but gifted baby-sitters—they're just so hard to find. I feel so guilty," she admitted. "Letting you help me when I'm the one who should be doing all those things with him."

Nathan grasped her chin with one hand to hold her still, then gently stroked her face with his thumb, staring into her eyes so that she'd know that his next words were true. "You'll do those things," he assured her. "When you get some time, when you get rid of me and get back to a less hectic schedule, you will. Because you love your son, you know his needs. You're a good mother, Faith. You are."

"And you're a good man, Nathan," she offered softly. "A very good man." But Nathan didn't reply. He couldn't. He knew she was wrong. If he was a good man, a truly good man, he wouldn't be standing here now. He'd be six feet under, the one who had taken the brunt of that crash. And his wife and child would still be alive, still offering the world their sunshine. A few childish games of Cootie with a wistful little boy, a day at the park flying a kite, couldn't wipe out the past. Nothing could.

The house was empty when Faith came home a few weeks later. The ticking of the clock emphasized the silence. She'd grown too used to Cory's laughter mingled with Nathan's deep voice, Faith realized. She'd taken advantage. Nathan's few days had turned into weeks. "The wind's not right for kites," Cory had said when she'd brought up the subject, and Nathan hadn't disagreed. But then he wouldn't. He didn't want to disappoint her child—or any child, she remembered. *She* should have been the one. *She* should have called Mandy and insisted that the baby-sitter return. Instead, she'd done nothing, treasuring the smiles Nathan brought to Cory's face. That was wrong. *She'd* been wrong, but she hadn't stopped to think. Now in the silence that marked Nathan and Cory's unexpected absence, she couldn't hide from her thoughts or her guilt anymore.

Passing the refrigerator, she saw a note hanging there. It was scribbled in big, red crayon letters—wobbly letters—some of which were backward. Obviously this had been a two-man job with Nathan spelling and Cory writing.

"Gone to the park," the note read. "Be back soon."

Wonderful. She'd have a few minutes of solitude, a commodity that was in short supply lately. She could put her feet up, have a cup of coffee, read a book... the possibilities loomed before her, beckoning. So why was she marching into the bedroom, pulling jeans and an old baggy red sweatshirt out of her drawer? Why was she pulling out her banged-up, used-to-be-white sneakers?

*Because she was crazy, foolish. Because she needed some real honest-to-goodness exercise. Because it was such a nice day. Because she loved seeing Nathan and Cory together....*

It was as simple as that. The big man, the small child, laughing, telling ridiculous, nonsensical jokes, then rolling on the floor as if they were really funny. Challenging each other to games, arguing over what was the worst vegetable in the world. Once she'd even found them sound asleep on the couch together, Nathan's shoulder cradling Cory's head. How could she resist? How could she stand to miss a minute, when she knew that the minutes were almost gone?

She couldn't, but neither could she let things go on as they were. It wasn't fair to Nathan. Besides, his therapy *was* almost at an end.

Locking the door behind her, Faith made her way down the sidewalk to the park at the end of the block. The orange plastic slides and bright blue tunnels were filled with kids, but none of them looked like her own. She didn't see Nathan's long legs anywhere, either. Shading her eyes she looked around. They weren't at the basketball courts, or in the sandbox, or even sitting on a park bench. Then, finally, she heard a distant squeal, and looked up to see her son jumping up and down as Nathan set a bright green kite soaring in the open space at the edge of the play area.

Faith moved forward, not watching where she was going, not taking her eyes off the two for whom she had been searching. Nathan played out the string, easily manipulating it between his fingers, grasping at it and jerking the kite higher when the breeze threatened to pan out.

Cory looked at the kite, then glanced back to Nathan, his adoration of the man clearly written across his face. It was a blow to her heart, that look. Nathan had won her child's loyalty, won him completely... just as he'd won her?

No, she wasn't going to think that, wasn't going to think about her own feelings at all. Instead, she turned to watch Nathan's hands. It was her job, it was what she was supposed to be doing, she reminded herself; not thinking about how big a hole her and Cory's lives would have soon. She wasn't supposed to be thinking about how much she'd miss standing up to the man, having him argue with her, tease her, touch her....

Unaware of her presence, caught up completely in what he was doing, Nathan gracefully, easily played with the string, twisting and turning his long, elegant fingers as he threaded the line out. He gripped the string, his fingers moving, letting out the slack, automatically answering the dance of the wind as the kite rose higher in the air. Nathan fed the line. Automatically. Easily.

She saw it then, what she'd suspected, though she'd told herself she needed more time to be sure. A therapist couldn't be too careful with a patient, couldn't push them out of the nest too soon. But now the truth was there, bold, undeniable, written in Nathan's easy grip and his careful control of the slender string. She couldn't turn away or deny what her eyes told her so plainly. She couldn't pretend he needed anything more from her.

Nathan was on his way, he was going back to the hospital. She'd been right before, the minutes *were* almost gone. She had done her job.

Nearing the two of them, she saw Nathan gently transfer the now high-flying kite to her son's small hands, and heard Cory call, "This is so fun, Nathan. I wish we could do this forever and ever."

Nathan turned to look at Faith as she approached. "I know what you mean, son. I know just what you mean," he said.

But Faith knew that his words didn't really mean anything. Because Nathan *was* leaving their lives. She was going to have to sever the connection—tonight. She'd talk to him tonight.

She'd been flitting around the kitchen like a butterfly gone berserk ever since Nathan had quickly finished going over his manipulative exercises. Faith knew she wasn't acting like herself. It wasn't like her to be this nervous . . . to avoid looking into his eyes when he turned her way. But she did just that very thing because she wasn't sure what she was feeling, and she didn't want him reading her expression when she didn't even know what was written on her face. This was no time to be emotional or confused. She and Nathan were on the homestretch of his treatment. Now, it was more important than ever that she be strong.

Nathan rose to leave after the session had ended and Cory had finally said his good-nights. He was smiling down at her, ready to say his own farewell, when she cleared her throat.

"Don't leave. Not just yet," she said quietly. "Wait until I put Cory to bed. I have a few things I need to discuss with you." Then she slipped quietly from the room, not allowing him time to reply, not giving herself time to decipher the stunned look on his face.

She was back in minutes, having promised a too-tired Cory a story the next day. By now Nathan's stunned look had turned to something else. He was staring at his hands when she came in, bending his fingers back and forth as if to test his strength.

*He knew,* she thought. *He knew what she was going to say.*

"So... Faith, are you—are you going to take me to task for taking Cory out of the house without asking your permission today?" he questioned, but she could tell by the skeptical light in his eyes that even he didn't believe that.

"No, not at all." She shook her head. "You left a note. Cory enjoyed himself. Why would I object?"

"No reason. I was just making sure I knew what this was all about, trying to tell if what I suspected was true."

Faith pasted a smile on her face, a phony smile, a professional smile, the kind she hated when she saw it on anyone else. But it was necessary at this moment. She was going to give him good news and confirm his suspicions— the long wait was over, he was almost home free. It was her job to tell him the truth and to be happy that he had reached his goal.

She *was* happy. She was near tears watching him as he flexed his fingers, knowing that he had his life back—at least a part of it. But for some reason she didn't want to try to understand, she couldn't come up with a completely ecstatic smile.

"You don't need me anymore," she said suddenly, as if she had just realized that for herself. "That's what I wanted to tell you. For some time I've known you were getting close, very close. Today, watching the way you handled that kite string with such unconscious grace, it was clear...well, it's absolutely obvious that you've arrived, Dr. Murphy. Or at least...almost arrived. You *will* have to ease back into things, I'm sure."

"Does that mean I'm not exactly ready to compete as a concert pianist yet?" It was a small attempt at levity, one Faith appreciated since she seemed alarmingly close to something that felt much too much like tears. And she couldn't allow herself even a single teardrop. She couldn't let her mixed feelings show. Only smiles were in store.

"Do—do you play the piano, then?" she asked. "I never knew."

"Never had a lesson in my life," he whispered. Stepping close, he took the hand that she was nervously twisting around the back of a chair. "I only meant that I'm not quite ready to open people up and solve their medical problems yet, am I, Faith? So, how can you be totally sure then that I don't need you?"

She opened her mouth, waiting to push back the lump in her throat before she spoke. "I'm totally sure," she managed in a voice that should have been stronger. "The little bit of ground you have yet to cover will happen. It's just a matter of time and continuing on with your exercises. In the meantime, you're more than ready to return to work on a limited basis, consulting and so forth, doing the prep work for what will soon follow. I wasn't lying. You really *don't* need me any more."

"So we're ending things tonight, then?" Nathan's voice was tight, his grip on her hand like an iron band—not painful, but unyielding. "Cold turkey, huh?"

Nathan watched Faith. Her dismayed expression at his words made his heart clench. But at least she wasn't wearing that steady, practiced therapist smile, the one that held him a broomstick's length away. The one that told him she was overjoyed. She'd finally accomplished what she'd set out to do, and was finally getting him out of her hair.

Well, what did he expect? She'd made it clear from the first that he was not a patient she wanted to take on. There was no reason for her to feel the way he was right now, as if something were twisting deep inside of him, tightening painfully. As if panic were about to explode in his chest.

Taking a long, deep breath, Nathan pulled himself up straight. Hell, what was he thinking? This was what he wanted, what he'd waited for, too. If the bright burst of ecstatic relief hadn't come yet, it was only because he hadn't been ready and waiting for it. It would come in time. Soon he'd wake up and realize that he finally had what he'd wanted from the start.

"Cold turkey, Nathan?" Faith was saying. And her voice was soft, confused, maybe even hurt. "No, no, of course I didn't mean, I *don't* mean for it to be that way. We'll spend the rest of this week getting you prepared for a return to your life, your career. I'll make sure you know what you need to do in order to be one hundred per cent effective when you step into the operating arena. I wouldn't desert you, Nathan, without making sure that you were really ready."

Her apologetic look, and the way he'd wiped that smile off of her face so readily, made Nathan feel like kicking himself. He was being a jerk to her again when he ought to be kissing Faith's feet. She'd come to him against her will, and managed to save his career. She'd given him something to occupy his mind other than the torturous thoughts that had almost destroyed him. How selfish could a man be, wanting her to feel badly about ending things? Hell, wasn't this what he'd wanted her to do, what he'd demanded she do? Get things over with as quickly as possible.

"Faith." He clutched the hands that she was holding out in supplication. "Faith, damn it. Stop apologizing to me. I sure as hell don't merit that. Besides, haven't you learned by now not to listen to anything I say? Don't you know what a bear I am? I've said so damn many unkind things to you. Too many. But a minute ago, when I made that crack about you sending me off cold turkey—I was joking Faith, just joking. And badly, too. Believe me, I would never, ever accuse you of being anything but the best therapist in the world. You brought me around in spite of the fact that I fought you till you practically had your back up against the wall. When no one else other than Dan was willing to stand up against me, you did—only you. So don't think I'm being critical. I'm just adjusting, that's all, getting used to the thought of being physically whole."

"And you're happy?" she asked, staring up at him wide-eyed and anxious.

Hell no, he wasn't happy. He'd probably never really know the true meaning of that word again. But he knew that she wasn't referring to his personal life, just his reaction to the fact that she was giving him the green light, sending him back to the career that had once meant everything to him.

"I'm happy," he said. It was a lie, a monster of a lie, but that was just because he hadn't had time to adjust, Nathan reasoned. In a few days, when he'd had time to assimilate the truth, when he realized that he was finally free and clear of Faith Reynolds and her little imp of a son—free of all the temptation they held—he was going to be insanely happy. At last the weight of Faith's presence was going to be lifted from his life.

"I'm happy," he repeated. "Thanks to you. So...if today isn't the end, when exactly are we severing the cord that binds us, Faith? When are we calling a halt to this thing once and for all?"

Faith hesitated, bit her lip. "We'll—let's plan on Friday," she said, her smile back in place. "That will give us time to wind things down and make sure that there are no loose strands."

"Friday...." The end of the week, the logical choice. "Make it Saturday and you've got yourself a deal." Nathan couldn't believe what he'd just said. There was no reason to press this thing further, he'd be much better off once he'd concluded this episode in his life. Besides, Faith *never* saw him on the weekends.

"Saturday?" Faith tipped her head back and looked up at him, her aqua eyes suddenly concerned. She worried the soft pad of her lip with her teeth. God, he wished she wouldn't do that, wished she'd paste the too bright smile back on her lips. "I'm afraid I don't understand, Nathan. Why?"

Nathan stepped nearer, closed his mind to good sense, and even managed a smile of his own. "Faith...don't question the inevitable. You told me once that gratitude was quite common between patient and therapist. If that's so, and this is the end of our road together, then I want one opportunity to show you my appreciation. These are my hands you've given me, not a small thing. Besides, I've promised Cory one more outing—it's just something simple, Faith. So don't look so worried. I'm not going to embarrass you."

"I wasn't thinking that—but I'm not sure—"

"Shh." He stepped forward so that he was up against her heart, so that she was tucked into the cove of his body. Silently he threaded his fingers through her hair, something he'd been wanting to do from the first. He wouldn't kiss her, not tonight. He wouldn't worry her again. But he had to feel these silky threads just once before it was all over and done.

"A simple outing, Faith. With you. With Cory. I started it all so wrong, pushing you around. I want to end it right. This will be our last time together. Let's end it with a bang, just the way we started things. Let me be grateful, Faith. Let me do this one thing."

Gently he touched his lips to her hair. It wasn't a kiss, not really, he told himself. Even though he felt the sigh slip through her body. Even though she was so soft and close against him that she felt like a part of him, her heart echoing the too-fast rhythm of his own.

"Nathan," she whispered, in a voice that shook with emotion. No, he told himself, that was just his imagination. He was projecting his own feelings onto her, making believe that this was as much of a wrench in her life as it was in his.

In a few weeks when they'd pass each other pleasantly in the hospital, it would be as if this time had never existed— for either of them. That was the way it should be, friendly, impersonal, not with him wanting to pull her tighter against him.

Abruptly he released her, half prepared to tell her to forget his suggestion. Making their last time together something special would be a mistake. It would make the adjustment period longer and more difficult.

He looked down at her, and for a fleeting moment thought that he saw pain. He closed his eyes, tamping back the fear that flooded through him. Of course, he had been mistaken. No way could he have been right about that. She was probably just feeling put-upon because he'd been touching her again when he'd once said he wouldn't. He couldn't bear to think he'd hurt this woman in any way. It was important to him that he leave her untouched, unscathed by his presence. It was why he'd fought so hard against her, why he fought so hard against himself to keep from touching her when all he really wanted to do was hold her, rain kisses down her throat, take her to his bed for long, slow hours of lovemaking.

The thought made him blanch. He'd never have that, wouldn't allow it. This whole idea had been crazy, foolish. He couldn't even stand next to her without thinking of her naked and beneath him, touching him, letting him touch her. One day more would only make things worse. Opening his mouth, Nathan prepared to take back everything he'd said and tell her that Friday would be fine, that they could call it quits tonight. Surely Dan could tell him everything he needed to know.

Faith suddenly rose up on her toes. She nodded, hard, cutting off his thoughts. "We'll end on Saturday, then," she said decisively. "You're right. It will be more final. I like things to be crisp and clean-cut when they end."

Her words brought him back to reality. She'd put a new twist on his suggestion. She wanted to make things more final. Well...so did he, didn't he? Of course he did. Things would be so much better for both of them, for all of them, once he had cut the ties that bound them.

They had to be better. He couldn't stand to see that pained look in Faith's eyes again. He didn't want to live with the fear that he had put it there. They needed to part, soon, before he really did hurt her.

Faith wandered through the house after Nathan left, picking up Cory's books and toys. She hadn't had the heart to make him pick up his things earlier. Not tonight when he was so close to losing Nathan.

Opening Cory's door, she peeked in as she always did. His breathing was slow and even, his mouth relaxed and open.

The night-light near his bed cast shadows on the wall, sending a ycllow puddle of visibility just as far as the dark corners that had once scared him so. Of course, those corners weren't so scary any more. Nathan had chased away the monsters. Faith wondered if they'd come back after the man who'd scared them away had gone.

She hoped not. She hoped Nathan's solution was a permanent one, not dependent on the man. Because, heaven knew, she couldn't contact him once he had gone. She and Cory couldn't be near him, ever again. She'd known that for certain when he'd wrapped her in his arms. She could say goodbye once and be brave. More than that was asking too much of herself.

Moving to tuck the sheet higher around Cory, Faith saw the wadded up bit of paper in Cory's clutched fist. His list. It was getting more pathetic looking every day, wrinkled and torn. But he was holding it as though he held pure gold, filled with the promise of something he wanted badly—so very badly.

Gently, she removed the paper from his grasp, found the fat, red crayon that had dropped and rolled up against his side.

She smoothed the edges of the paper, making it flat. The eraser marks she'd made just a few days ago were still visible, the missing words beneath still faintly readable. Only a few items remained. *Not afraid of kids or monsters. Doesn't have to be good at Cootie.* But it was the last thing on the list that gave her pause and made swallowing difficult. Her eyes misted and she had to blink hard to keep the tears from falling. On the paper, written in her neat handwriting were the words *Not a doctor.* The word "Not" had been crossed out with a red crayon.

She remembered Cory asking her to point to the words, realizing now why he'd needed to know. *A doctor.* The words seemed to scream at her. *A doctor.* Cory wanted a doctor for his daddy.

No, Cory wanted Nathan. He wanted only Nathan.

And God help her, so did she.

She loved Nathan Murphy, in spite of all she knew; that *she* didn't want love, that *he* didn't want love. That he couldn't love *her* or anyone as long as his past held him prisoner. But none of that made any difference to the way she was feeling right now. She loved him, like it or not.

Faith *didn't* like it, not at all, but she knew it was true. Just as she knew that somehow she had to get through the next few days. Because then, only then, she could begin again, begin learning how not to love Nathan.

## Chapter Eight

Saturday had arrived in a split second it seemed, the week galloping away too quickly. Still, Faith was determined to be cheery, to handle the farewell to Nathan this evening like she would any other patient's swan song. Firmly, she took herself in hand. She rose early, busied herself making a big breakfast and planned activities for her and Cory. They would clean, they would go to the park, they would play games, read, draw, enjoy themselves.

It seemed like such a simple plan, easy to implement, bound to be effective. But by early afternoon, she and Cory had done all those things, some of them twice. Frantically and without fun. The day was dragging, and Faith was angry with herself for feeling that way, for wishing the hours would spin by so that Nathan—

"Mom?" Cory's voice, loud and demanding, appeared out of left field, tearing her away from her thoughts.

"What, tiger?" she asked, turning to him. "You want to know the time again? It's a whole two minutes since you asked me last. Maybe not even two minutes," she said, smiling indulgently. She looked down at her son who was sitting cross-legged next to the coffee table, wielding a green crayon and sliding his tongue along his lips as he worked on the picture he was drawing.

"No, mom. I know it's gonna be a whole long time. You to'd me. I just want you to spell somepin' for me. How do you spell *big*?"

"*Big*, huh?" Faith raised one brow in surprise. Cory had always rather balked when she'd worked on his letters with him before, and he'd certainly never asked her how to spell anything in the past. "All right, well, let's see. That's *b* then an *i* and then a *g*. You know, the circle with the tail on it."

"*B*," Cory said as Faith carefully repeated the letters several times more. Finally, satisfied, he breathed out a sigh of relief. "Okay, now *yellow*. How do you spell *yellow*?"

Once again Faith named the letters slowly.

"Cory, what are you writing, anyway?" she asked, trying to lean over and see.

"Nothin', Mom, just one more word. Okay? One more?"

Shrugging, she nodded. "One more or as many more as you need, Cory. Just tell me what the word is."

"It's—*hair*."

Faith's eyes met Cory's determined ones. She saw now that he had put his drawing aside, saw what he was actually working on, the word *Big* scrawled in green beneath her own neat handwriting. When she realized that the next line would say *Yellow hair* when Cory had finished his painful printing, her first inclination was to protest, explain the way things were to him again. Instead, she carefully spelled the word. It would do no good arguing. She'd already told him Nathan couldn't be his father, the man on that list. He knew that it was so, and still it didn't matter. She knew that nothing she could say would dissuade him right now. Only time and Nathan's absence would do the trick.

Time away from Nathan was what they both needed. But there was still today.

And her own heart was just as stubborn as Cory's. She still wanted this day with Nathan, one day to hold close. One more day to store up memories that would have to last a lifetime.

He came with roses, big bunches of them. They were blush pink, the color of Faith's cheeks when she got up a good steam. It had been his first thought when he'd seen them at the florist, and he brought them because he'd promised her he would, because they reminded him of her... because a woman like Faith should have flowers... often. Not because he was trying to win her or tell her anything special. He wouldn't do that, but still...

"They're for remembrance," he told her, placing them in her arms when she opened up the door. "And, of course, for gratitude." He managed to work up a half-smile. "Maybe just for putting up with me, for not spitting in my eye and slapping my face when you should have."

*That's it, Nathan,* he reminded himself. *Keep it light. Keep it breezy, uncomplicated.*

"I remember. They're to celebrate the end," she said, her words reminding him of what he'd told her so many times.

She was right, that was what they were supposed to be doing tonight. Celebrating the time they'd spent together, the fact that they would no longer be compelled to share any time at all. Because she had done her job so well. Because he'd worked so hard.

But standing out on the miniature golf course a scant hour later, surrounded by bright plaster animals, whirling windmills, and scads of families out to enjoy the warm weather, Nathan wondered why this didn't feel anything at all like a celebration.

No, that wasn't the truth, he admitted, turning to look at Faith as she watched her son gripping his golf club. He *knew* why this didn't feel like a celebration. It was Faith. She was just too damn beautiful, standing there in the breeze, the wind lifting her hair from her neck, tossing it around her shoulders. The white shorts and bright jade blouse she wore snugged against her curves the way a man's hands would—should. She was achingly alluring...and he was never going to see her this way again.

Forcing himself to look away, he turned to the little boy beside her. Cory's scrawny little limbs thrust out of his blue T-shirt, his elbows two sharp points as he bent his arms and prepared to swing the golf club with complete abandon. Again.

"Whoa, partner," Nathan said, stepping forward and stopping Cory's motion. He bent over the tiny boy, curving his body close to guide him. "Like this. Nice and easy," he instructed. "Let's put it right through the rabbit's mouth. You can do it. Just take your time. That rabbit's not going anywhere."

Cory chewed on his lip. "But it's almost the last hole," he whispered. "I gotta do good this one, Nathan. I gotta show you that I can do better than sixes." He turned to Nathan then, his eyes big and round and anxious.

Faith started to step forward, but Nathan waved her back. Gently he took the golf club from Cory's clenched fists. He tapped one finger against the child's nose.

"Hey buddy," he said, going down on one knee. "You don't have to prove anything. You're the Cootie champ. But even if you weren't, even if you weren't the champ of anything, you and me would still be pals. Wouldn't we?"

At Cory's solemn nod, Nathan gave him a wink. "Okay, then Cory, just give it your best shot. That's all you have to do."

Carefully, Cory took aim and swung. The ball racketed into the rabbit's mouth, looped around the bright blue metal curves twice, then moved onto the green. Heading for the hole, it veered aside slowly, missing the cup by three inches.

"I missed," Cory said glumly. "I missed again."

"Shh, son, it was a great shot. You got closer to the hole than I did. Now just give it a little tap this time."

Cory did as he was told and this time the ball went right in the cup.

Nathan held out one big hand and Cory slapped his palm against it.

"Cory, Cory, that was great," Faith called. "You got a birdie. An honest-to-goodness birdie."

She held out her arms for a hug and Cory moved closer, dark eyes shining. Just before he reached the shelter of her arms, he picked up one of her hands and gave it a hard slap.

"I did it, Mom," he agreed. "I got a birdie. But," he turned slowly, looking toward the next hole, the last hole, the end of the game. "But maybe I should do it again, try for a hole in one. Maybe we could play again. It's still early."

"It *is* still early," she agreed, "but I have to tie up a few loose ends with Nathan before he goes. How about ice cream back at the house before we say goodbye?"

Nathan looked at Faith in surprise. He hadn't realized they were going to the house, thinking they'd say their goodbyes in the parking lot. Here, where it was open, public. A place where he wouldn't be tempted to think and do and say things that were unwise.

But Faith wasn't looking at him, wouldn't look at him, just as she hadn't since they'd left the house. And then, at last, Nathan understood. When Faith had said that she wanted things to be crisp and clean and final, she'd been thinking about *him,* worried that like other patients she'd probably had, he wouldn't be able to say goodbye easily.

Faith had already written him out of her life. She was just worried that he would have difficulty doing the same.

As he came back from returning the clubs to the booth, Nathan studied Faith. Her back was to him, giving him a perfect view of shiny hair, a sweetly curved bottom, and the delicious length of her pale, bare legs. She was lovely and any man who saw her would want to touch her. But it was a simple lift of one hand, the way she turned to her son and gently smoothed his hair, that made Nathan's heart lurch, that told him she'd been right in her assumption.

He was going to have trouble saying goodbye to Faith Reynolds. She'd be in his thoughts for a long, long time.

Silence reigned in the car on the way home. Several times Faith thought she felt Nathan looking her way, but she kept her eyes on the scenery, knowing she would be lost if she caught his gaze. Her feelings were too near the surface, they'd be readable no matter how hard she tried to hide them. She had to end this completely and not give herself away. She had to be all business from here on out.

Once they were home, Faith carefully dished out bowls of ice cream, then sat down to join Nathan and her son. Cory, she noticed, was listlessly pushing the vanilla ice cream around his bowl. He ignored the chocolate sprinkles he'd always loved.

She turned to Nathan. "All right, prepare yourself," she said. "It's time for the speech. The one that's supposed to rev you up and keep you going on your own. Don't think for one second that you can stop doing your exercises, just because you don't need a therapist anymore. You'll still need to practice every day, every night, to maintain your flexibility until you're back on the job one hundred per cent. You understand that, Nathan? You can't get lazy. And it's up to you to police yourself, to discipline yourself to that regimen, to keep yourself from falling back into bad habits. Because I won't be here to crack the whip over your head, and I don't intend for you to backslide. I mean it, Nathan. I really do," she said when he smiled at her no-nonsense tone.

He leaned across the table, pushing his own bowl out of the way. "So, this is why you brought me back here?" he asked, smiling straight into her eyes. "To lecture me?"

She looked back at him, solemn as she shrugged apologetically. "I couldn't humiliate you in public, Nathan."

His laugh was low, never sexier. The green of his eyes was dark, tempting her to lean closer.

"Oh Faith, I'm going to miss you. You and your prim schoolteacherish orders, your lion tamer tactics...." He sat up straight, blowing out a breath and, finally, looking away, freed her from his mesmerizing gaze. "I don't know, Faith. Trying to keep you from losing that fiery temper of yours was a great incentive for working my hands. You alone kept me going at times. Without you there..."

Faith rose from the table suddenly, crossing her arms as she frowned down at him. "Nathan Murphy, I'd better not hear of you slacking off or closing yourself up in that house again. Not once. If I do, I'll..."

He moved silently, quickly, got to his feet and stepped to her side, stopping so close that she couldn't breathe deeply without brushing against his skin. "What will you do, Faith? Storm my door again? Set your tent up outside my house the way you once threatened? Beat your lovely fists against my chest? You'd be surprised, Faith, to learn how much I'm going to miss that bossy side of you."

And she was going to miss him, all of him, Faith thought. Caught off guard by Nathan's nearness, the sudden strength of her emotions, Faith closed her eyes to keep Nathan from seeing the pain that she knew must be clearly stamped on her face.

Immediately, he stepped back, and held out one hand. "That wasn't an insult, Faith," he said, misunderstanding her concern. "I was teasing. I really do admire you, you know. There's no finer therapist, I wouldn't have had any other. And you don't have to be concerned. I'm going back to work. No more hiding away. No more letting things go. I wouldn't do that to you, I wouldn't let you down that way."

He touched the back of his fingers to her chin, ran his knuckles against her skin. "So, I guess this is it then," he whispered. "Time for me to do my disappearing act?"

"Nathan?" Cory's voice was a sudden, high-pitched sound across the table.

Faith looked up to see her son, his eyes large and watery, his ice cream a forgotten puddle of brown and white in the bowl.

"Don't leave yet, Nathan, okay? I got somepin', somepin' I need to show you. Will you stay? Will you stay?"

"Shh, Cory, don't worry. I didn't mean I'd go without saying goodbye. And I wouldn't go, *won't* go until you're back. I promise you that."

Cory bit his lip, nodded as he hopped off the chair and ran from the room as if the monsters had returned. When he came back, he held something crumpled so tightly in his fist that at first Faith didn't recognize it. When she did, her heart froze, a lump the size of Chicago formed in her throat.

"No, Cory," she said, reaching out. "Go put that away, sweetheart." But it was too late. Cory launched himself at Nathan, shoving the torn bit of paper into Nathan's big hands.

"Nathan," she said, moving to take it from him. She couldn't bear for him to read it, couldn't bear for Cory to throw his heart to the wind this way. "It's not—don't read it."

But he was already reading it. The words that Faith knew so well swam before her eyes. *The Daddy List. Not afraid of kids or monsters. Doesn't have to be good at Cootie. A doctor.* And Cory's latest additions. *Big. Yellow hair.*

She blinked rapidly, zoomed in on her child's face. Cory was watching Nathan read, his hope, his love written in his eyes, as obvious as the red and green crayon on the list. And Faith knew that she'd let this go too far, much too far, that she should have stopped things long ago.

Turning to Nathan, she tried to think of a way she could explain, help him know what this was, what he needed to say that would make this easier for Cory.

"It's—it's—"

"The Daddy List," he whispered, his husky voice stumbling over the words.

Nathan looked up at Faith, saw the fear written on her face, saw her concern for her son. She needn't have been afraid. He'd go through fire and flame before he'd do anything to intentionally hurt that wide-eyed innocent sitting across the table.

"Cory?" he managed, his voice broken.

"It's my list," Cory explained in a small, painfully small voice. "My Daddy List. Mommy and me, we're looking for a daddy, someone to marry us up and live with us forever. We need a daddy real bad. We need a daddy to come and be our own, a daddy that wants us bad."

Nathan's heart did a somersault, his mind froze into ice cubes. "You need a daddy," he repeated. "You do," he said as if realizing it for the first time. "Well son," he whispered, "I hope you get the very best daddy in the world. Because any man, *any* man, would be lucky, really lucky, to have a boy like you."

A tentative smile broke through the tension that wreathed Cory's face. "Then," he swallowed. "Then would you—"

"Cory," Faith drawled out the word, soothingly, stopping his speech, holding out her hand as she started around the table toward her son. "We talked about this, remember, and I told you—"

"I know. I know." Cory was rocking on his toes, swallowing hard, rubbing his arm across his eyes. "I know what you said, that Nathan could not be my daddy, but—but I didn't ask *him*. And you always say you'll never know if you don't ask. I gotta ask, Mom. I gotta."

Whirling, Cory turned and flung himself toward Nathan. "You could be our daddy, Nathan. I wouldn't win so many games at Cootie. I'd let you win sometimes, honest. I would."

The tears were streaming down the little boy's face now, unheeded. His whole body was trembling.

Nathan closed his eyes. *My God, what have I done to this child?* he asked. *Please, don't let me hurt him. Don't let me hurt another child.*

Slowly, Nathan moved closer, and sank to his knees. He pulled Cory onto his lap and wrapped his arms around the tiny, shaking body.

"Cory," he managed, his own voice weighted with tears. "Cory, I didn't know you wanted a daddy. I didn't know you wanted one so much or I wouldn't have come and made you hope. Because, you see, Cory, I can't be anybody's daddy right now. I lost my own little girl not so long ago.

I'm afraid I'm not good daddy material any more. I couldn't be anyone's daddy," he repeated.

Cory pushed tighter into the haven of Nathan's body. "But I could wait," he wailed. "I could wait until some day, when maybe you could be a daddy," he promised.

Nathan shook his head, squeezing Cory tightly. "No, Cory," he said, pulling back then. "It wouldn't work. I just can't do it. I can't be a daddy. But—" he continued at the child's protest.

"Cory," he said, thumbing the tears from the little boy's eyes. "If I *could* be anyone's daddy, I would be yours. You would be the boy I'd want to have. The way things are, though, I hope you know that I'm always going to be your friend. I always want to be your friend, your *good* friend. Even if I'm not always around, I'll be that for you. All right?"

The little boy stared up at him, snuffling softly.

"Friends, Cory?" Nathan asked, holding out his hand for Cory to slap it.

Cory bit his lip. When he finally reached out to Nathan, he grabbed his hand instead of slapping it. He took Nathan's hand in both of his small ones. "I guess so," he finally said, a defeated tone in his voice.

Nathan took a deep breath. He closed his eyes once more, hoping that Cory hadn't been ripped apart too much.

"Come on, sweetheart," Faith soothed. "It's time for bed. It really is much later than you should be up. Say—say good-night to Nathan now."

Nathan steadied the little boy as Cory climbed off his lap, took his mother's hand and turned to go.

They were almost out of the room, moving slowly when Cory turned back.

"I got—I got a birthday in two weeks," he whispered. "I'll be five—big then. Big boys don't cry, Scotty Miller says."

Sucking in air, Nathan stared back, blinking hard. "Scotty Miller is wrong," he said. "Big boys do cry. And Cory, I'll remember that birthday. I would never forget."

When Faith returned, she looked tired. And wary. Her blue green eyes were dark. Her gaze wavered when their eyes met. Then she looked away entirely.

"I—I'm sorry about that," she said. "He's been having some hard times in school lately. Feeling left out without a father."

"A boy *should* have a father," Nathan said, watching for her reaction.

She nodded, swallowed hard, placed her fingers over her lips as if to guard her words, then slowly let them slip away. "I know. That's why we started the list. I just didn't know it would turn out this way. But don't worry. It's changed dramatically in the last few weeks. After you're gone— after he's used to you being gone—we'll make more changes."

"You'll look for someone to marry?" Nathan could barely force the words out. The thought of Faith searching want ad style for a husband, the thought of hordes of men, all kinds of men, passing through here, and trying to win a place in Faith and Cory's life—he didn't want to carry that thought to its logical conclusion, but it happened anyway. In time there would be someone, one man, who would belong here. And that man would have the right to Cory and to Faith, to her time, her days... and all her nights.

"You'll marry," he said simply.

Faith bit her lip. "Like you said, a boy should have a father."

"And a woman should have someone to hold her at night?" It was true, so damn true, even if the thought of someone, any someone other than him, sharing Faith's nights, made Nathan's breath stick in his throat.

Hot color flooded her face, and she raised one hand to her chest defensively.

"I'm sorry," he said, reaching out. "That's none of my business." It wasn't, and he'd damn well better remember it.

She started to shake her head, but he stopped her, resting his hand on the small of her back, hating the fact that she flinched when he did it. "Faith," he told her, "don't pay any attention to me. I'm sorry—especially about Cory. I guess I wasn't thinking how this was going to affect him—"

"No. Don't," she said. "If you weren't thinking, I was. And I let it happen anyway. I don't know why. I shouldn't have. I knew he'd never understand that this had to end. He's never met any of my patients before. He doesn't know about beginnings and endings."

Nathan looked down into Faith's face. For a moment she seemed wistful, open. He thought of that damn list, that list that meant some day soon another man would stand here with her at times like this when she was upset. Another man would be able to comfort her properly, to take her in his arms, take her lips and kiss her long and deep. Another man . . . one who deserved her, who'd never have to worry about hurting her the way he would. A man who wouldn't fail her. And that was what she deserved, what he wanted her to have; another man, a good man.

So why in hell did he feel more helpless than he'd felt before Faith came along? Why did his hands feel so empty and useless?

He didn't know, but he wasn't going to think about that now. No way. Angrily, he pushed back his thoughts.

"I meant what I said about Cory's birthday, Faith. And don't worry," he quickly added, when he saw the troubled look in her eyes. "I won't come back and open the wounds, but I'll send something. I couldn't stand to have him think that I'd just forgotten him like that. He's special, he really is. And little as he is, he's helped me—so much. When I first came here, I used to tremble at the sound of the word *kid*. He got me past that. Tell him...someday. All right? He should know, but not just yet."

Faith nodded, keeping her head turned to the side.

"Well, I guess I should go now," he offered. "Do you think that Cory's asleep?"

"I—yes." She turned, a concerned look in her misty eyes as she agreed. "I'm sure he is. He always goes right off, especially when he's upset. It's a kind of solace for him."

Nathan hesitated, clenched his fists at what her words meant, then plunged on. "Then—do you think—would it be all right if I looked in on him once before I go?"

Faith took a deep breath, let it out on a trembling sigh, then nodded. She moved to the room and quietly opened the door.

Nathan stepped inside. The room was dark except for the small circle of light that illuminated the far corner. Moving closer, Nathan gazed down on the small shadowy form on the bed, noted the places where the blanket outlined the thin legs, the bump that was Cory's teddy bear. Bending low, Nathan gently touched the dark hair that lay across Cory's forehead.

"Nathan?" The sleepy little voice wound its way around him. Two little arms snaked out from beneath the covers and wrapped around his neck. Cory squeezed his face up against Nathan's neck and held on tight.

"Nathan," the half-sleeping boy said, as if he had finally come home, could finally rest. "Nathan, you're here."

"Shh, Cory. Go back to sleep."

With tears behind his eyes, Nathan drew Cory close, hugged him once, gently, then eased him back onto the bed. Faith followed him as he left the room.

*Deep breaths, Nathan. Deep breaths, don't think.*

And he didn't. He couldn't, could only act. As soon as the door was closed, he turned, pulling Faith into his arms, levering her high against his body, fitting her lips to his own.

His kiss was hungry, fierce, hard. He plunged his hands into her hair. Held her tightly as she wrapped her arms around his neck and kissed him back. For the last time, he knew. The last time.

"It's time, isn't it?" he whispered against her lips. "It is," he agreed, answering his own question as he loosened his hold on her, sliding her down until her feet were on firm ground. Gently he let her go and stepped back.

She looked at him for long seconds, then slowly nodded. "It's late," she agreed. "Nathan?" She raised one hand, touched the front of his shirt. "Don't blame yourself for Cory. Don't let him become another regret, something you can't forgive yourself for."

It was too late for that. He knew that, but chose not to say so. He *already* had regrets about Cory—how could he not—but at least he hadn't hurt Faith. At least he had left *her* intact.

"I—" She led him to the door, holding out one hand as if she didn't know what to do. "I guess this *is* the final goodbye, then," she said. "This is really the end."

A silent scream tore through Nathan's heart, begging him to stay. But he pushed it back, knowing he had to get away.

He'd be a fool to listen to his heart. Not when he knew all the facts. Not when he knew that if he could just leave, he'd be okay—in time.

At least he hoped so. Looking at Faith now, and then remembering Cory and those little arms that had clutched at him moments ago, Nathan wondered how big a piece of his heart he'd lost to this woman, this child. Maybe it wasn't as big as he thought. Maybe it just felt that way right now, because he was leaving. Perhaps it was just that he was facing the separation for the first time, and feeling the gratitude that Faith had always told him about.

She could be right.

She *wasn't* right. This couldn't be gratitude that he was feeling. This need to reach down and pull her close to tell her he wanted to stay with her and help her raise her son was more than gratitude, more than mere desire. He only hoped that time away from her would help, that he'd soon forget.

"Nathan?" she asked. "Don't forget—don't forget to take care of yourself, will you? Please?"

He picked up her hands in his own strong, healthy ones. "I won't forget," he promised. *Not any of it. I won't forget you, sweet Faith. Even though I want to.*

"I'll remember Cory's birthday," he added, moving out the door. "I gave him my word, and I'll keep it."

He was gone—really and truly gone. Out of her life.

Faith paced the confines of her kitchen, holding her arms tightly against herself, not sure she could hold together otherwise.

Nathan was gone, she'd set him free. And she realized at last that she'd been hoping, desperately, that at the last moment, he'd decide not to go.

*Fool.*

Faith pressed her hands to her mouth, stifling the cry, the sob that tried to crawl up her throat and escape. She leaned her forehead against the kitchen window, feeling the cold, unforgiving glass against her skin.

Where was Nathan right this minute, and what was he feeling? Relief? That's what he'd always said he'd feel when things were finally over. Maybe even joy once he had time to think about it.

He certainly wasn't feeling love. Never love. He'd made that clear all along, he was no longer a man who loved.

For a moment there when he'd come out of Cory's room and kissed her so desperately, she'd actually hoped. But no, that was something else. It had been a reaction to the fear that he'd hurt her and Cory. Perhaps it had been desire, as well. It wouldn't have been the first time Nathan had touched her and passion had flared.

Relief. Regret. Desire. But nothing more. Because even after reading Cory's list, he'd gone. And he wouldn't be back.

Faith's knuckles turned white as she pressed them hard against the glass.

He wouldn't be back. She had to live with it, and go on with her life—for her and Cory. She had to go on as if Nathan had never crept into her heart, as if Cory had never asked him to be his daddy.

She had to accept the fact that she'd done what she'd promised herself she wouldn't do; she'd given her heart to a man who didn't want it.

At least he didn't know that. And that had to make a difference. If there was any consolation to be had in this evening, it was that.

In the morning she would pick up the pieces and go on. She'd begin to try to coax Cory into changing his list. She'd actually start making plans to *do* something about that list.

Somehow, she'd find a man for herself, and a father for Cory.

*A woman should have someone to hold her at night.*

Nathan's words slipped into Faith's thoughts, jarring her, shaking her. The mere thought of a man holding her at night, a man who wasn't Nathan... her heart spun.

Who was she kidding? How could she think about finding a father for Cory when the mere thought of another man touching her made her feel dizzy and sick?

Faith turned away from the window, and moved to the table. She picked up the dirty dishes that were still sitting there, then put them down again. All right, so she wasn't ready to go one-on-one with a man... yet. She would do something else. She *had* to do something else.

Somehow she had to move on.

The answer came bright and early next morning.

"Mom?" Cory wandered from his room, bleary-eyed and barefoot, dragging his teddy bear behind him.

Faith looked up from the place at the kitchen table where she had finally landed early in the morning. She hadn't slept, and it felt like a heavy stone had lodged in her chest. Somehow she dredged up a pitifully small smile. "What, love? Are you ready for breakfast?"

Cory, ignoring her question, kept walking until he was standing close by her side.

Faith pushed his sleep-tangled hair away from his forehead, and looked down into his worried eyes.

"Mom, could we maybe, you know, invite Nathan to my birthday party? He said he wouldn't forget it."

Taking a deep breath, Faith shook her head. "I'm sorry, Cory, but that wasn't what Nathan meant when he said he wouldn't forget. He can't be here that day. Besides, I thought you were only inviting kids."

Cory nodded, his eyes silently pleading, his toes wiggling against the linoleum. "I know, but Nathan—"

"No, Cory, no," Faith repeated gently, tipping his chin up so that he would pay attention. "Nathan *won't* be here."

The mention of Cory's birthday party struck a faint, but welcome chord within Faith. She *wasn't* ready to begin dating yet, couldn't even think of it. But maybe she could ease into things somehow. It had been so long since she'd been socially involved at all. Maybe if she started slowly, in a nonthreatening situation where she wasn't forced into face-to-face contact with one man... maybe it would be a start. A tiny start, but all that she could handle right now.

Faith looked down into Cory's waiting eyes again. "What if I invited all your friends' families, really make it into a big, special party?" she asked. "Would you like that? It might be fun, don't you think?"

Cory shrugged and sucked in his lip.

Well, what had she expected? He was hurting. Really hurting. Nothing was going to change that overnight.

"Cory?" she whispered, pulling him closer to her.

"That would be okay, Mom," he said dully as he pulled away. "And maybe if we told Nathan there wouldn't just be kids—"

Framing her son's face with her hands, Faith gazed into his eyes. "We have to forget Nathan, Cory. We have to."

The furious look Cory gave her lanced through her like a sharp sword, making her gasp. "I don't want to forget Nathan," he said, wrenching himself away and running back to the safety of his room. "I don't want to forget Nathan *ever.*"

Faith wanted to go comfort him, but she didn't. He needed to be alone right now, and besides, what could she say? She knew how he was feeling, because she didn't want to forget Nathan, either. Still, she had to. She was at least wise enough to know that . . . and to know how difficult it was going to be.

Her only hope was that the pain would ease a bit by the time Cory's birthday had arrived. She prayed that her son would find some small amount of happiness in a day that ought to bring only joy.

In the meantime, she had to keep going...somehow. She had a party to plan, a life to plan. One that didn't include Nathan Murphy.

# *Chapter Nine*

A full week and more had passed, but Nathan had not made the kind of progress he'd anticipated, at least where forgetting Faith was concerned. He was back working at the hospital and had seen Faith several times from a distance. Each time he looked her way his system short-circuited.

Now here she was again. He could see her at the far end of the hospital corridor he and Dan Anderson had just entered. Faith was talking to Bill Neely, a tall, blond orthopedic surgeon. It was business, of course, Nathan told himself. Neely was a wild one, not the kind of man Faith would want. She was probably consulting with the man about one of his patients.

But that damn list kept floating before Nathan's eyes. Big. Yellow hair. A doctor.

Maybe she *was* consulting about a patient—or maybe not. By now she'd be searching for Mr. Right, and he couldn't blame her. She'd be looking for a man to build a life with for her and Cory, and that was the way it should be.

"Nathan? You there, Nathan?"

Dan Anderson's voice slowly sank in and Nathan turned to him, frowning. "Did I miss something?"

"Yeah, only everything I've said...for about the tenth time in two days. Look, Nathan, why don't you go talk to her? It's obvious you want to, that you're worried about her."

"About Faith? Get real, Anderson. Faith's a good, strong woman. I have it on the best of authorities. You told me that yourself when you sent her to me."

"Sicced her on you, you mean. And yes, she is strong. And capable...and a thousand other wonderful things. But if you're not worried about her, then how come your hands clench like vise grips every time another man walks near her?"

Nathan felt his jaw tighten, knowing he'd been too transparent. "They don't."

"Right, you just normally go around brandishing iron fists. And don't try to blame that on a problem with your hands. I know better. I also know that we *are* going to have a problem if you don't get your mind off your beautiful therapist and back on Mrs. Wyndham's surgery."

"Ex-therapist," Nathan mumbled. "She's my ex-therapist. And I'm not worried about her. I'm just... grateful. I'm just thinking about how grateful I am to her."

Dan looked at Nathan as if he'd gone insane, which was pretty damn near to the truth. In spite of the fact that he was back on the professional track again, Nathan felt as if he *had* lost it at times these days...every time he saw some man sidle up next to Faith. Every time he thought of her, which was sure as hell too often.

This had to stop. *He* had to stop. After all, she had a right to a life that didn't include him. Because he had nothing to offer her. He was a man whose emotions were still in pieces, who was chained to his past.

Nathan stared hard at Faith, knowing his thoughts were pointless. She had been his therapist, and that was all she ever would be. He wouldn't be doing her any favors by trying to hold on to her, and if he so much as even dimmed the light in those lovely blue eyes—no, he wouldn't do that. At least he wouldn't if he could just stay away.

Sucking in a breath, he turned to Dan, and held out his hand for Mrs. Wyndham's charts. "All right, Dan, tell me again about the patient. I'm listening this time. You've got my complete attention."

Dan stared at him, shaking his head in disbelief. "Even if I tell you that Dr. Lowden is stopping to talk to her and Neely?"

Nathan's gut tightened, but he forced himself to hold his hands still, managed not to clench them into fists. Joe Lowden was the newest doctor on staff; talented, caring and an all-around nice guy. He was also ridiculously handsome... and he loved children. He was the perfect man for someone like Faith.

"Give me the file, Dan," Nathan said, too quietly, ignoring his friend's incredulous look. "And stop staring at me like that. I'm only interested in three things right now. Work, work and work."

But it wasn't work he was thinking about two days later when he saw Faith coming toward him down a hospital corridor flanked by Joe Lowden again. Hell, it wasn't work he'd thought about for days, for almost two weeks. He should be diving in headfirst, rediscovering that supreme commitment that had won him the respect of his peers ...

and wounded his family. But all he'd been able to think about was Faith. Faith and Cory.

Now, seeing her with Lowden, watching the way the man leaned close to her, Nathan started to seethe. Trying to control his thoughts. he forced himself to remember that Lowden would be good for Faith, that he himself should have every reason for wanting her to find such a kind, caring man.

Instead, he stopped dead in his tracks. She did, too.

Looking him full in the face for the first time in two weeks, Faith turned all her attention from Dr. Lowden to Nathan. She was a good twenty feet away, but he saw her open her mouth as if to speak, then close it again.

It didn't matter. Nathan's gaze was riveted to her face. He saw her eyes widen. Felt the moment the connection was made between them.

Faith stared at him, the blind that had kept him from seeing what he'd been afraid of dropping completely. Her lips trembled. Her eyes, those beautiful, haunting blue green pools that had darkened often with anger when he'd fought her, softened now, turned liquid with longing, with...

Nathan took a step back and away. Closing his eyes, he felt the shudder go through him as he forced himself to breathe, to come to grips with what he was seeing. Her heart, her soul, laid out for his inspection. His to have—or to harm. Nathan sucked in air at the enormity of what Faith had revealed, knowingly or otherwise. And deep inside, he felt something else. Relief.

But when he opened his eyes, Faith's face was shuttered, closed to him. Her shoulders were rigid. She stood taller. The softness in her had flown, and her eyes—it was as if he'd turned to glass and she could look through and beyond him.

Slowly, she turned to Dr. Lowden, giving him all her attention as they continued down the hall toward Nathan.

Only five steps away, Joe nodded, an acknowledgment of a fellow colleague, but Faith's gaze was fixed squarely on her companion.

"Faith." Nathan called her name softly as she neared him.

She looked up and nodded her head in greeting. "Dr. Murphy, I'm—pleased to see you back on staff," she said, not pausing long enough to stop.

It was the politest of responses, professional in every sense...and it made Nathan's blood start to heat with frustration, especially when Faith walked away with Lowden.

Turning, Nathan forced himself to watch them move down the hall into the distance. He saw the way Lowden flattened his hand on the small of her back to turn her toward an open doorway. It was a touch a husband—or a potential lover—might use. Nathan saw Faith stiffen, though she didn't move away.

Nathan gripped his fists tight, not caring who saw the action this time.

Faith wasn't in love with Joe Lowden—at least not yet. No, she cared for *him*, Nathan. He'd seen it in her eyes, on her lips. But...it didn't matter, she wasn't going to let it go any further.

As the sounds of the hospital flowed around him, as people came and went, slipping past him in the hallway, Nathan stood there, and faced reality. He realized what he'd been hiding from all this time, since the day she'd first pushed him to the edge. Faith Reynolds held his heart, every shredded bit of it.

Faith was the woman he loved...and he couldn't have her. He'd lost her, bullied her, turned from her, told her he didn't want a family. And no matter what she felt, she wasn't going to come to him, not when he was still haunted by his private ghosts. She wouldn't ask a man like him for tomorrow when she knew that he was still buried in yesterday.

Instead, she was going to take that damn list and go looking for the perfect husband and father—a man who was heart-whole and steady. It could be Joe Lowden or someone else who wanted her and Cory so badly he'd do whatever he had to just to hold them and keep them.

That was the kind of man Faith *should* have, someone who'd battle any obstacles to be with her and make her happy, a man who would stand up to anything for her. A man who loved her more than he feared facing his own demons.

In that moment, Nathan knew without question that he wanted to be that kind of a man. He just wasn't sure if it was possible. The past had a strong hold on him, and he'd have to fight for all he was worth if he ever intended to be free of his yesterdays, if he ever hoped to have anything to offer Faith.

Standing at the table, Faith surveyed the pile of decorations she'd been sorting through—streamers, banners, balloons in eye-popping shades of marigold and electric blue. This should have been a time of excitement, she should have been gearing up for tomorrow's party. So why was it so hard to smile?

A small shadow flitted through the room behind her.

"Hey, tiger," she called, to Cory. "Want to help me pick out the things that we need to really jazz up this place?"

He sidled up to her slowly, the same way he'd been behaving for the past couple of weeks. Obedient, but without enthusiasm, he'd trudged along, pretending at play.

And he hadn't mentioned The Daddy List. Not once in all that time.

"So, what do you think?" she asked, smiling a bit too brightly. "Is this pizzazz in a box or what?" She held up a sparkly Happy Birthday banner for Cory to see.

Cory managed the smallest of smiles, touched the dangling banner with one finger. "It's nice, Mom."

Faith stifled the frown she felt forming. She wasn't going to ask him what was wrong. There was no need. Cory had the same problem that she did. He missed Nathan. But there was nothing to be done about that. The situation was unfixable, hopeless, and she'd only made things worse today.

How could she possibly have done something so stupid as letting down her guard and allowing Nathan to look into her heart? It only made things so much worse, so much harder to bear. Especially knowing that he'd seen what she was feeling and, had chosen to step away from her, closing his eyes to shut out her love. Faith had to bite her lip even now to keep back the gasp of pain. She'd risked what she'd promised she'd never risk again, risked it all—and come up empty. The past was repeating itself. Only this time the pain was ten times sharper, a hundred times deeper. This time the man was Nathan.

"Hey, tiger," she said softly, taking a deep breath and gently tweaking the end of Cory's nose. "Don't you worry. We're going to have a great time tomorrow, you and I. Wait and see. Everyone's coming to celebrate your big day. Why, even Scotty Miller's father called to say that he *would* be in town and could come after all. Our house will be hopping—and I'll bet you get lots of neat presents, too."

She'd tried to give him everything he'd asked for, and had most likely succeeded since he'd requested so little. But there was one thing she couldn't give him—the one thing he wanted most.

Because Nathan was gone. Gone for good, she reminded herself, forcing herself to resume the party preparations and smile at her son. Tomorrow the house would be filled with people, guests she needed to meet and entertain. And this party was meant to be happy, to cheer Cory up and help her get over Nathan and back into the world. She and Cory were finally going to take the first step and look for the husband and daddy they needed. And this time they would do it right. This time they would make sure they found someone they liked—not someone they loved.

Nathan lay in the sweat-soaked darkness, listening to the thudding of his heart. And waiting, waiting for the memories to take hold, the ones he'd pushed away for almost two years.

Visions of Faith intruded, and Nathan groaned, wanting nothing more than to pick up the phone and hear her whisper his name. Just once.

But no. He wasn't going to contact her, wouldn't even go near her again. Not yet, not while he wasn't complete and free. Not until he put the past to rest.

Remembering the past would be a risk. It would mean opening himself up to revelations that could break him completely. How much *was* he willing to risk for the woman he loved?

Silence. Darkness. Mere seconds passed. Then slowly, intentionally, Nathan turned. He moved to pick up the picture of Joanna and Amy he'd left by the side of the bed. He forced himself to look at the moonlit photo and to breathe deeply. The thought of Faith, her eyes soft and swimming with the love that she'd turn from and offer to someone else, made Nathan's blood pound furiously in his veins. Slowly he opened his mind, his heart, and finally, fully summoned the demons of the past, allowing them to rise up around him.

He was awake, never more so, yet this time he didn't run from the waking nightmares; instead, he turned and faced them. He saw his Amy, laughing and bright, telling him that she loved him. Joanna, sad with dark, accusing eyes. Joanna telling him that he loved his work more than her, that he was too dedicated to helping other people when he should be helping her. His own arguments that he couldn't turn away from people in need. Her tears. His regrets that he couldn't be more what she wanted.

Nathan grasped a handful of the bed sheet with each hand. He felt the onslaught of pain inside his heart. Hot pain that intensified, spilled over, running into the night of the accident.

Memories pressed in on him. Darkness. The road lit by eerie lamplight. A sudden roar as a car rushed through the red light, coming at them in a swerving, reckless path. Tires squealing. Trying to turn, spin the wheel, slamming his foot on the accelerator as he pushed to get out of the way of the careening vehicle. Impossible. Impossible. Screams. Joanna's. Cries in the nightmarish darkness. *His* cries—tears and panic clogging his throat. Then searing physical pain as he reached to help his wife. Metal hot and sharp, twisting against his hands.

He'd tried. Oh how he'd tried to save her, save them. Tried to get to his child, to claw his way deeper into the wreckage and breathe life into her when it was already draining away. He'd tried.

He'd failed.

The pain was too great. The pain would never leave...but through the pain, he could see her. Faith. Lovely, sweet, giving Faith. He'd lived through the pain for her—faced it at last. And he'd do it again if he had to.

He had tried to save his family, he realized now. And while it was true that he hadn't been able to save their lives, it was also true that the accident hadn't been his fault. He couldn't have changed things, couldn't have done more than he had. The other car had been moving too fast.

Nathan sank back into the softness of the rumpled bed. He ran damp palms over the tangled, sweaty sheets.

His heart was racing, hammering, pounding. The dreams were too close, the ghosts of the past too near. But *he* wasn't a ghost, he was a man.

He'd lost, lost badly. But as the dark settled in deeper, all through the night, and even into the burgeoning dawn when the first streaks of light lit the sky, Nathan made contact with the truth, touched on memories both vivid and real. He made peace with his demons.

Finally, with shaking fingers, he picked up the picture again, gazing at the wife and child he'd adored. He held it close, moved his thumb over faces he'd never see again.

As the sun began its trek into the sky, Nathan said farewell to the woman he'd tried to love. He brought the photo close and kissed his daughter goodbye.

He wished Amy could have met Faith. She would have liked Faith. His Faith.

*His* Faith . . . if it wasn't too late.

But it wasn't going to be too late. Couldn't be.

Rising, he hunted out the smudged crayon-decorated birthday invitation Hannah had picked up and passed on to him. He knew the invitation had been sent without Faith's knowledge. He hadn't meant to attend the party, planning to merely send a present and a note.

Now nothing on earth could keep him from the woman and the child he loved. Somehow, someway, Nathan knew he had to convince Faith that he *was* the man on the list, that he was a man she and Cory could count on through eternity and beyond.

The house was the same as Nathan remembered, except for the balloons and the big Happy Birthday Cory sign that covered the front door. He pulled the Suburban halfway up the block—as close as he could get with all the other cars parked there. Then, taking a deep breath, he reached for the long, slim package in the back seat. Fumbling with the door handle, he eased his frame out of the car.

Long seconds passed while he stood there. He could hear the sounds of a party going on, people laughing, talking, kids squealing. He listened for Cory's voice among the squeals, but couldn't find it.

He'd hurt the boy that last day, remembering so clearly the small arms that had hugged him close, practically begging him to stay. Nathan's own heart gave a painful lurch at the thought, and he promised himself he'd never hurt Cory again. He'd never leave him again, if he could help it. If Faith would open her door to him.

Quickly he walked up the path, kept walking, steadily, constantly, straining until he heard it. The sound of her voice.

Nathan raised his head instantly, and saw Faith was in the backyard, talking to a handsome, dark-haired man. She handed him a string of bright patio lights as she reached to hang the first one herself. The man smiled at her, and pulled the hammer from her hand. He took over the job himself and said something in a low, teasing voice, something Nathan couldn't make out.

No matter. He saw the smile cross her face, saw the way she leaned closer to answer. Her hair, honey-toned and soft, brushed the man's shoulder. Her beautiful hair that Nathan remembered so well. The kind of softness a man wanted to tangle his fingers in as he kissed her, touched her, loved her.

Sucking in his breath, Nathan felt the jealousy, hot and bubbling, boil within his gut. He swallowed hard, forcing himself not to move or do something foolish.

He was here for a reason, and he wouldn't be able to explain himself if he flattened the nose of one of Faith's guests.

Nathan ran one hand over his tense jaw, took a few steps closer. He was nearing the gate now. In another minute, he'd be inside, he could see her, talk to her.

"Cory, Scotty," the dark-haired man called, finishing the stringing of the patio lights. "Come here."

And as Nathan watched, Cory and another little boy, curly-haired like the man, ran up to the adults. Reaching out, the man ruffled the other little boy's hair, and did the same to Cory's. Then, as Faith called for someone to plug the lights in, he picked up both boys, one in each arm. He held them high so they could see as the red, green and yellow lights came on, glowing in the gathering darkness.

Faith reached out and touched Cory's arm. She smiled at her son and at the man, who was beaming back at her possessively.

A family, Nathan thought. They looked like a family.

He should leave them alone.

But as he stood there, a present in one hand, the fingers of the other hand bunched tightly, Nathan could almost hear Faith that first day, chastising him for not trying. He took one more step forward. To hell with the man in the yard. There was a woman and a child inside that fence whom Nathan loved, and he couldn't just walk away.

"Faith, I've got to try," he whispered. He couldn't give up without a fight. As sure as he'd lived when he might have died, as sure as he loved Faith heart and soul, he couldn't walk away.

Squaring his shoulders, narrowing his eyes, Nathan arrowed his way straight to the gate, flipping the latch in one quick move. The last time he was here, he'd been a patient struggling to retrieve his career. Now he was a man out to win a woman, the only woman that mattered. And nothing—neither man nor monster—had better stand in his way.

Faith looked up when Nathan came through the gate. Tall, broad shouldered and imposing, his green-eyed gaze sought her out and pinned her where she stood.

She started to step forward then stopped, her heart beginning a slow, hard thud that felt as if it would tear her apart.

Unable to speak, she simply stood waiting.

Nathan took a step closer.

Faith tried to breathe. She forced herself to reason with her pounding heart. He was holding a present, a gift for Cory that he'd give to the boy and then leave, this time forever. It was important to remember that, to kick away from the need to throw herself into Nathan's arms. She couldn't do what she wanted and ask Nathan to come back to her and Cory.

Cory. She could hear his voice coming from the other side of the yard where he and Scotty had run off with Mr. Miller. Cory shouldn't see Nathan. This wasn't right. She didn't want her child to end his birthday in tears, even though she knew that *she* was going to do that very thing.

Her thoughts melted her frozen limbs like sunshine on ice. Quickly she moved forward to meet Nathan, to intercede, to stop her son from seeing him.

"Hello, Faith." Her name flowed from his lips like a husky caress, but of course that was only what she wanted to believe.

"Come inside, Nathan," she whispered, taking his hand and leading him away from the lights of the backyard.

But as soon as they crossed the threshold of her house, as soon as they were safely locked away from Cory's view, she dropped his hand quickly, as if she'd found herself holding a still glowing ember.

Faith turned to face him, trying to ignore the mesmerizing heat of his gaze. "Why are you here? You can't be here," she told him, forcing herself to cross her arms and harden her features.

A slow smile crossed his lips. He dropped the package on the counter, leaned closer, and she noticed that his long, blond hair was as shaggy as ever, as touchable, as enticing.

She held out her hands as if to fend him off.

Instead he leaned even nearer, ignoring her hands as he brought his lips close to her ear. "I love it when you turn to flame, Faith," he whispered. "And don't tell me I can't be here. I *am* here, as you can see."

And suddenly stepping back to give her room to breathe, Nathan leaned against the doorjamb. He crossed his ankles, his arms, as if he intended to stay that way forever.

"You haven't answered my question, Nathan." Faith fought to keep her voice stern, tried to close her mind to all the wicked things his presence was doing to her nerves. "And I don't want you here. We've said our goodbyes, you and Cory and I. I don't want him to see you. He can't see you here, Nathan," she pleaded, closing her eyes as he shifted and the warm, male scent of him drifted close.

"Faith..." His voice was like a touch, nearby, but still too far from her. "I *couldn't* stay away, though heaven knows I tried. Besides, I promised Cory I wouldn't forget his birthday. Did you think I'd break my word to him? Do you think so little of me?''

She could sense the moment he moved away from the door frame, felt the second he arrived back at her side. His voice drifted near, slipping over her like warm fingers, pulling at her, hurting her because she knew he'd be gone so soon. This was just a moment in time that would be snatched from her any second. And she hated knowing it was so easy for him to leave her while it was all she could do not to beg him to hold her.

Faith took a full two steps back from Nathan. She forced herself to look full into his face, wanting him to know how much she wished he'd leave. Now.

"Nathan, please, don't you remember that last night when we said goodbye? Didn't you see how it was for Cory, have you forgotten that list? You can hurt him so easily, Nathan. So... please go. Aren't you worried about hurting him?''

She saw him blink, falter once when she mentioned the list, as if she'd convinced him to go. But then he stepped forward, cupped her chin in his hand, leaned close.

"I am worried, Faith," he admitted. "More than you know. And no, damn it, I haven't forgotten the list. It's been in my thoughts... constantly. That's why I'm here, why I'm back when you know darn well I didn't mean to come here in person and upset Cory again. I'm here because of that list you and Cory made. Because if I remember correctly, I happen to meet the requirements. And I'm here to apply for the position of father—and husband." His voice was low. He slid his thumb over her lips as he spoke.

Faith couldn't control her trembling mouth. Nathan was touching her, stroking her.

She tried to step back again, but found she was only inches away from the wall, and Nathan followed her there in a slow waltz.

Swallowing, she shook her head. Only yesterday she'd given up all hope of Nathan ever caring for her. Now he was here, telling her he wanted to be her husband. But...why? Because he felt badly about hurting her son?

It wouldn't work. It wasn't enough. With another man things would be different. But with Nathan—she couldn't marry Nathan without love. No matter what she'd planned. No matter what the damn list said.

Slowly, Faith slid her hands down to grip her skirt, clenching her fingers in the bright folds. She shook her head again. "I don't want you here," she reiterated. "I want you to go. I want you to leave now."

Nathan reached down and gathered her clenched fists in his own large hands. Gently he stroked, coaxing her fingers to uncurl. "No way, Faith. We've played this game before. The day you first came to me." He slid his thumbs across the sensitive skin of her palms, caressing her flesh, warming her with his own heat.

"And Faith," he continued on a whisper as he leaned near, bridging the small space that had kept her body separate from his. "I hope you remember the next line. Only this time it's mine. As you once told me in so many words, I came here tonight for a reason. A simple yes from you is all I need, all I want."

There was nothing in the world Faith wanted more than to believe that Nathan was offering to marry her because he cared. But she'd seen him step away from her before, she'd witnessed his reaction to her naked feelings.

"Nathan, if you're worried that you're somehow responsible for us—for Cory and me—I didn't mean to make you feel that way. That list, please, forget it. You don't have to be concerned. I don't *want* you to be concerned. You're not responsible for us. In any way."

He moved away then, far enough so that she could see his face clearly, could look into his eyes. He turned her palms up so that her hands rested on his own.

"And what if I want to be responsible for you, Faith?" he demanded, his voice turning harsh. "What if I've found that the surgeon with the magical fingers has no magic at all without you?"

She looked away to hide the hope in her eyes because she couldn't allow herself to believe what she was hearing. She'd heard the same thing from other patients. It was gratitude again, she reminded herself, simply the first pangs of separation.

"That's just the reaction to trying to find your way again at the hospital," she whispered, hating the fact that her voice sounded small and scared. "That's all it is."

"No, Faith, no." Nathan slid his hands up her arms, beneath the fall of her hair, as he pressed closer, surrounding her body with his own. "No, Faith, that's not gratitude, it's not me finding my way, it's not any of those things. It's love, Faith. It's the love within me talking."

She tried to open her mouth and he stilled her with a kiss. "Faith please," he began, "let me say the words. I love you, completely. I realized how much that was true when I saw you yesterday, and I've been half out of my mind wondering if I've lost you. What's more, I'm jealous, sweetheart, so damn jealous of every man who comes near you. I'm jealous of that man outside and I have to ask. Have I waited too long? Do you still care for me at all?"

Faith jerked her head up. She opened her mouth, determined to deny that she cared, had ever cared. If she could only protect herself, keep herself from hurting when he came to his senses. . . .

"Don't," he whispered, stopping her words with a touch of his finger to her lips. "Don't say it, don't deny what was between us. I *know* there was something, Faith. I do, because I spent so much damn time trying to run from it. And then yesterday—" Nathan looked at her with such fierce desire that Faith leaned forward involuntarily, swaying against him.

"Yesterday?" she choked out.

Nathan brought her tighter against his hips, slipping his hands up beneath her hair. "Yes—in the hospital—seeing you looking at me like that, with love. And don't say that you weren't. We both know that you're not a liar. In those few seconds, I knew that whatever you felt for me, no matter how powerful, you were going to ignore it. You were going to walk away to protect me from the pain you thought I'd feel. Do you know how much that scared me, sweetheart? It shook me, rocked me, completely. I'd worried so much about not deserving you, about losing you some day because I'd killed any feeling you might have for me. I—just never considered the fact that I could lose you *because* you cared for me.

Faith sighed and raised her eyes to his. He'd found her out, knew her secrets. There was no hiding this time. But still she pressed her hands to his chest, as though that small defensive gesture could protect her from her own emotions. "I never wanted to care," she whispered. "Not again and certainly not this strongly. I didn't want to ever feel something this overpowering, but—" She took a breath, shrugged, nearly managing a watery smile. "What can I say, Nathan? I just don't seem to have much control over whom I love, or even how much I love, because—heaven help me—I *do* love you. So much, so very much. I'd hoped it didn't show so clearly."

Nathan gathered her close. He wiped away the wet path of the tear that trickled down her cheek. "It shows, Faith," he said, his own voice suddenly thick. "But only to someone who returns that love so completely. I've spent the last two days saying goodbye to the past, finally admitting that I didn't have the power to save my wife and daughter and that I hadn't really failed them the way it felt I had."

Catching her breath with relief, knowing that Nathan had taken a step away from his painful past, Faith rested her head against his chest and sagged against him.

"Faith..." Nathan groaned, banding his arms more tightly around her. "Don't be sad. Because—nearly losing you, knowing you'd let me go in order to save me from myself—it made me realize a person can't hide from the pain. There's no way. Pain comes with the love. So, don't walk away from what you feel for me. Please. I love you, completely. And it's forever, Faith."

Faith looked up then, straight into his eyes, smiling through her tears. Sliding her arms around his waist, she moved as close as she could get. "Then that love must be the same kind I feel for you, Nathan, the kind that never goes away, no matter what. I'll love you forever and always. And—" She paused, suddenly self-conscious.

Nathan lifted her up to him. He teased her lips open with his own as he kissed her hungrily, nipping at the sensitive skin.

"And?" he whispered, when he finally moved a breath away.

Faith felt the hot color rushing into her face. "And you needn't have been jealous of the man outside. Or any other man. That's Scotty Miller's father. Scotty is one of Cory's friends."

"That's good, then," he whispered, bringing his lips to hers again. "I didn't really want to spoil the party by planting my fist between his eyes."

"Nathan?" Faith pushed back and gave him her stern therapist look. "Don't you ever go hitting another man for my sake. I absolutely abhor violence and I don't want Cory to see something like that. Besides, I worked way too hard on those hands to see you mangle them on some other man's nose just because you thought he was going to—"

"Marry you, Faith?" he asked, trailing kisses down her neck. "That's what I thought, what scared me so much," he murmured. "The thought that some other man might have earned the right to hold you, touch you, love you the way I want to—I—" His hands tightened around her waist. "Be my wife, Faith," he urged. "Be mine forever."

"I want to," she agreed on a whisper. "I want to say yes. But Nathan, I'm not alone. I need to, have to, know what Cory is to you. I remember your fears about children."

Nathan's smile was slow and strong as he cupped her face with his hands and stared into her eyes. "Cory?" he asked. "Cory is my son, definitely my son. Maybe not by blood, but by right of love. That is, he will be . . . if you agree to marry me."

"I—" Faith opened her mouth to speak, just as the kitchen door swung back in a wide arc.

"Nathan! Nathan!" Cory hurled himself against Nathan, hugging his knees.

"Billy Wilkin's daddy told me that a man who looked like you was with Mom. What are you doing here?" the child demanded. "Mom said you couldn't come, so why are you here?"

Faith watched as Nathan smiled. He let his fingers drift over her son's hair and closed his eyes tightly. Then loosening Cory's fingers, Nathan reached down to scoop him high into his arms.

"I'm here," he said simply, "because I love you and your mom. If she agrees, we'll get married. That means we'll all be together. Forever, son." He hugged the little body close as Cory wrapped his childish limbs around Nathan's neck.

"It means something else, too," Cory said solemnly.

"What's that, Cory?" Faith asked, watching her son and the man she loved together, closer than clouds and sunshine, smiling, happy with each other. She swallowed over the lump in her throat.

"I'll show you," Cory said, wiggling down and running from the room.

Faith barely had time to exchange a puzzled look with Nathan before Cory was back. He held a shredded piece of paper, one she knew so well.

"If you marry us up," Cory said, his voice low and serious, "it means we can tear up The Daddy List. We won't need it any more. Not if you're our daddy."

Without speaking, Nathan reached over to take Faith's small hand in his own large, strong one. His hand, the one he saved lives with, the one she'd restored to him.

"Aren't you going to say yes, Mom?" Cory asked, jumping up and down. "Aren't you supposed to kiss Nathan or something?"

Nathan laughed and with a tug, brought Faith tumbling against his chest. "Aren't you going to say yes, Faith? Aren't you going to kiss me?"

She looked up at him, knowing that it was all right from now on to look her fill, to touch as much as she wanted. It was all right this time to love with her whole heart.

"Say yes, Faith," Nathan whispered once again.

And rising on her toes as Cory tore the Daddy List into bits and tossed it in the air, Faith wrapped her arms tightly around Nathan's neck. Her toes left the ground as he held her against him.

"Yes, Nathan, definitely yes," she said as a miniature confetti cloud drifted about them. "Yes, Nathan, I'll marry you. I'll always love you."

"Me, too," Cory added.

And as she and Nathan moved apart, enough to let Cory in for a hug, Faith looked at the man who loved her. This love, she knew, would last until the end of time.

*     *     *     *     *

# HE'S MORE THAN A MAN, HE'S ONE OF OUR

## THE WOMEN IN JOE SULLIVAN'S LIFE
### Marie Ferrarella

Joe Sullivan had enough on his mind with three small nieces to raise. He didn't have time for a relationship! But Joe couldn't deny the attraction he felt for Maggie McGuire, or the way this compelling woman cared about his sweet little girls. Maybe Maggie needed to love these little girls as much as he needed her, but it would take some convincing....

## COMING IN AUGUST FROM

FF895

## SOMETIMES BIG SURPRISES COME IN SMALL PACKAGES!

# BABY TALK
### Julianna Morris

Cassie Cavannaugh wanted a baby, without the complications of an affair. But somehow she couldn't forget sexy Jake O'Connor, or the idea that he could father her child. Jake was handsome, headstrong, unpredictable...and nothing but trouble. But every time she got close to Jake, playing it smart seemed a losing battle....

Coming in August 1995 from

**Silhouette ROMANCE™**

BOJ3

**He's Too Hot To Handle...but she can take a little heat.**

# FLYAWAY VACATION SWEEPSTAKES!

This month's destination:

## Glamorous LAS VEGAS!

Are you the lucky person who will win a free trip to Las Vegas? Think how much fun it would be to visit world-famous casinos... to see star-studded shows...to enjoy round-the-clock action in the city that never sleeps!

The facing page contains two Official Entry Coupons, as does each of the other books you received this shipment. Complete and return all the entry coupons— **the more times you enter, the better your chances of winning!**

Then keep your fingers crossed, because you'll find out by August 15, 1995 if you're the winner! If you are, here's what you'll get:

- Round-trip airfare for two to exciting Las Vegas!
- 4 days/3 nights at a fabulous first-class hotel!
- $500.00 pocket money for meals and entertainment!

Remember: The more times you enter, the better your chances of winning!*

*NO PURCHASE OR OBLIGATION TO CONTINUE BEING A SUBSCRIBER NECESSARY TO ENTER. SEE REVERSE SIDE OF ANY ENTRY COUPON FOR ALTERNATIVE MEANS OF ENTRY.

VLV KAL

**FLYAWAY VACATION**
SWEEPSTAKES

## OFFICIAL ENTRY COUPON

This entry must be received by: JULY 30, 1995
This month's winner will be notified by: AUGUST 15, 1995
Trip must be taken between: SEPTEMBER 30, 1995-SEPTEMBER 30, 1996

**YES,** I want to win a vacation for two in Las Vegas. I understand the prize includes round-trip airfare, first-class hotel and $500.00 spending money. Please let me know if I'm the winner!

Name_____

Address _____ Apt. _____

City               State/Prov.          Zip/Postal Code

Account #_____

Return entry with invoice in reply envelope.

© 1995 HARLEQUIN ENTERPRISES LTD.                    CLV KAL

---

**FLYAWAY VACATION**
SWEEPSTAKES

## OFFICIAL ENTRY COUPON

This entry must be received by: JULY 30, 1995
This month's winner will be notified by: AUGUST 15, 1995
Trip must be taken between: SEPTEMBER 30, 1995-SEPTEMBER 30, 1996

**YES,** I want to win a vacation for two in Las Vegas. I understand the prize includes round-trip airfare, first-class hotel and $500.00 spending money. Please let me know if I'm the winner!

Name_____

Address _____ Apt. _____

City               State/Prov.          Zip/Postal Code

Account #_____

Return entry with invoice in reply envelope.

© 1995 HARLEQUIN ENTERPRISES LTD.                    CLV KAL

# OFFICIAL RULES

## FLYAWAY VACATION SWEEPSTAKES 3449

### NO PURCHASE OR OBLIGATION NECESSARY

Three Harlequin Reader Service 1995 shipments will contain respectively, coupons for entry into three different prize drawings, one for a trip for two to San Francisco, another for a trip for two to Las Vegas and the third for a trip for two to Orlando, Florida. To enter any drawing using an Entry Coupon, simply complete and mail according to directions.

There is no obligation to continue using the Reader Service to enter and be eligible for any prize drawing. You may also enter any drawing by hand printing the words "Flyaway Vacation," your name and address on a 3"x5" card and the destination of the prize you wish that entry to be considered for (i.e., San Francisco trip, Las Vegas trip or Orlando trip). Send your 3"x5" entries via first-class mail (limit: one entry per envelope) to: Flyaway Vacation Sweepstakes 3449, c/o Prize Destination you wish that entry to be considered for, P.O. Box 1315, Buffalo, NY 14269-1315, USA or P.O. Box 610, Fort Erie, Ontario L2A 5X3, Canada.

To be eligible for the San Francisco trip, entries must be received by 5/30/95; for the Las Vegas trip, 7/30/95; and for the Orlando trip, 9/30/95.

Winners will be determined in random drawings conducted under the supervision of D.L. Blair, Inc., an independent judging organization whose decisions are final, from among all eligible entries received for that drawing. San Francisco trip prize includes round-trip airfare for two, 4-day/3-night weekend accommodations at a first-class hotel, and $500 in cash (trip must be taken between 7/30/95—7/30/96, approximate prize value—$3,500); Las Vegas trip includes round-trip airfare for two, 4-day/3-night weekend accommodations at a first-class hotel, and $500 in cash (trip must be taken between 9/30/95—9/30/96, approximate prize value—$3,500); Orlando trip includes round-trip airfare for two, 4-day/3-night weekend accommodations at a first-class hotel, and $500 in cash (trip must be taken between 11/30/95—11/30/96, approximate prize value—$3,500). All travelers must sign and return a Release of Liability prior to travel. Hotel accommodations and flights are subject to accommodation and schedule availability. Sweepstakes open to residents of the U.S. (except Puerto Rico) and Canada, 18 years of age or older. Employees and immediate family members of Harlequin Enterprises, Ltd., D.L. Blair, Inc., their affiliates, subsidiaries and all other agencies, entities and persons connected with the use, marketing or conduct of this sweepstakes are not eligible. Odds of winning a prize are dependent upon the number of eligible entries received for that drawing. Prize drawing and winner notification for each drawing will occur no later than 15 days after deadline for entry eligibility for that drawing. Limit: one prize to an individual, family or organization. All applicable laws and regulations apply. Sweepstakes offer void wherever prohibited by law. Any litigation within the province of Quebec respecting the conduct and awarding of the prizes in this sweepstakes must be submitted to the Regies des loteries et Courses du Quebec. In order to win a prize, residents of Canada will be required to correctly answer a time-limited arithmetical skill-testing question. Value of prizes are in U.S. currency.

Winners will be obligated to sign and return an Affidavit of Eligibility within 30 days of notification. In the event of noncompliance within this time period, prize may not be awarded. If any prize or prize notification is returned as undeliverable, that prize will not be awarded. By acceptance of a prize, winner consents to use of his/her name, photograph or other likeness for purposes of advertising, trade and promotion on behalf of Harlequin Enterprises, Ltd., without further compensation, unless prohibited by law.

For the names of prizewinners (available after 12/31/95), send a self-addressed, stamped envelope to: Flyaway Vacation Sweepstakes 3449 Winners, P.O. Box 4200, Blair, NE 68009.

RVC KAL